Love In Lansing
BOOK ONE

Searching *for* Anna

a novella

Jenifer Carll-Tong

JENIFER CARLL-TONG

philo se
PUBLISHING

WOULD YOU LIKE A FREE BOOK?

Would you like to stay up to date with all the latest news and upcoming releases? Sign up for Jenifer's newsletter and receive the Searching for Anna ebook as a free download! Visit https://goo.gl/Qur2sU today!

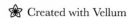

DEDICATION

In memory of Kenneth Stephen Busick...
for his tireless patience with the 14-year-old me, his limitless enthusiasm for literature, and his genuine encouragement of this budding writer. He was the first person to show me that writing wasn't just a dream, it could be my reality.

"It is not possible to know how far the influence of any amiable, honest-hearted duty-doing man flies out into the world, but it is very possible to know how it has touched one's self in going by."
~ Pip, Great Expectations

PROLOGUE

Tea for Three

*L*ansing, Michigan 1905

BAD THINGS HAPPEN to good people. Good things also happen to bad people, and Warren wasn't certain which was the greater injustice. He also wasn't certain under which category he fell, but he thought he was about to find out. He lifted his hand to knock on the massive, wooden door.

"He's in a meeting, Master Warren."

Warren's hand dropped to his side as he turned toward the butler. "That's unfortunate," he said with a smirk. He turned to leave, intent on a quick exit.

"Your father told me to keep you here until he is finished. He said it was imperative that he speak with you."

Imperative. That was one of his father's words for 'I'm going to kill that boy.'

Warren turned back to the servant. He was giving Warren the look.

"Don't even think about it, scalawag. You'll only delay the inevitable."

No other employee would speak to the seventeen-year-old son of his employer like this, but Jameson had dealt with Warren's mischievousness since he was five. He glared at Warren, confident that the boy would not disobey him.

"I'll be waiting in the drawing room," Warren sighed. Respect for one's elders really was a pain in the neck.

Warren sauntered into the drawing room and plopped down on one of the stiff settees, hoping to catch a quick kip before his execution. It wasn't the most comfortable piece of furniture in the house, but it reminded him of his mother, so he often found himself draping his lanky limbs across its small frame. He threw his arm across his eyes in a feeble attempt to block the afternoon sun that broke through the clouds and rested itself across the same settee.

"Hello."

Warren fell off the couch with a thud. He gathered himself onto his hands and knees and looked about the room, searching for the source of the tiny voice. He found it in a little princess of a girl seated across the room. Her pale pink dress, laden with rows and rows of ruffles, blended so perfectly with the muted shades of the mauve chair that had it not been for the abundant amber curls atop her head, she might have disappeared completely within the fabric. The chair, not overly large but much larger than the child, framed her like a throne as if she was holding court in the drawing room.

"Well, hello there," Warren said, pulling himself onto the settee. "Who are you?"

"I am Annabelle Grace Gibson. Who are you?"

Grace. She certainly has a lot of that for a child, Warren thought.

"I'm Warren. Warren Mallory. It is a pleasure to meet you, Annabelle Grace."

"Likewise."

Warren bit the inside of his cheek. As comical as he found the little girl's propriety, he didn't dare laugh and risk hurting her feelings. "So tell me, Grace, what brings you to my home?"

"My name is Annabelle Grace."

"Yes, yes. Of course," he smiled.

"I'm waiting for my father. He is in a very important meeting with a very important man that lives here."

My father, Warren thought. "Well, I don't know how important he is, but I'm waiting to see the same gentleman."

She sat in the too-large-for-a-child chair and swung her legs back and forth. Each swing of a leg caused her head of ringlets to bounce up and down like buoys on Lake Huron near the Mallory summer home on Mackinac Island. In her lap, she held a doll with hair the same color as her own.

"I don't know if you've noticed, but your doll isn't wearing any clothing."

The little girl blushed and looked down. "I tried to take the dress apart. I wanted to make it into an evening gown, you know, so she could go to a fancy party if ever she was invited. Taking the dress apart was easy, but I couldn't put it back together."

"What's her name?"

"Gertrude."

"Gertrude?" Warren repeated with a grimace.

"Yes, Gertrude. My father brought her home from Germany. Gertrude is a perfectly perfect German name."

"I suppose you are right." Warren smiled at the reprimand. "She looks like you, you know, but not quite as pretty."

"You think I'm pretty?"

"Yes. Very much so."

"Do you want to court me?"

Her question was too much for Warren to restrain his laughter. When he finally calmed, he looked back at the child to find her watching him, very much confused.

"Mother said that when a boy thinks a girl is pretty, he courts her." It was a statement but was posed more like a question. Warren ran his hand across his face in an attempt to wipe away any trace of smile. He rose from his seat and stuffed his hands into his pockets.

"That is very true," he said, strolling across the room. "But don't you think we are rushing things a bit? I mean, we've only just met."

"That's true." The little girl stared at the ceiling. She pondered this for a moment then turned her large, amber-colored eyes that matched the color of her hair to Warren. "But you think I'm pretty and I think you are very handsome, so what are we to do?"

"That is a quandary." Warren leaned against the doorway and stroked his chin dramatically. "I think the only solution for a pretty girl and a handsome boy is to have tea together. Would you like that?"

"Oh yes!" she said, the large bow on her head bobbing up and down. "Mother always offers tea to her guests, and I am your guest, so tea is a splendid idea!"

So, with that, Warren found himself in a tea party with Annabelle Grace and Gertrude. He had never served tea to a guest, and since his mother's death there had been very few female visitors to warrant practice in the art, but Annabelle had a great amount of knowledge on the subject and freely dispensed advice on the matter. Warren found it especially adorable when she informed him that children were always served the special tea that was found in the small teapot. He was confused until she pointed with a tiny finger toward the creamer pitcher.

"Do you take sugar in your 'tea'?" he asked as he filled her cup with milk.

"Yes, please. I'll take two."

Warren sat back in his chair and watched the little girl daintily stir the contents of her cup then tap the spoon delicately on the rim twice before taking a sip of the concoction. He pretended to sip his whenever he needed to hide a smile from something she said or did. He didn't care much for tea, but he was certainly becoming a fan of this little snippet.

They had just begun discussing the finer details of the game Cat's Cradle when they heard shouting. Warren knew the walls of the house to be rather thick. Whatever was being discussed in his father's study, it wasn't going well. He looked at his little visitor who had become silent for the first time since he fell off the settee. He started to speak but was interrupted by the sound of a slamming door ricocheting throughout the hall.

"Where is my daughter?" an angry voice asked someone, presumably Mr. Jameson. Before an answer could be given, the little girl ran to the doorway of the drawing room.

"I'm here, Father." She turned and curtsied to Warren. "Thank you for the tea, Mr. Warren Mallory."

Warren bowed in the most gallant way he could imagine, hoping he appeared as prince-like as possible. "The pleasure was all mine, Princess Grace. And we must do it again very soon."

His response seemed to please the little girl, sending a bright pink flush to her china doll cheeks. She waved furiously as her father whisked her out the door, grinning the entire way. Warren stuffed his fists into his pockets and smiled, shaking his head. He couldn't think of a more pleasant way to have spent his stay of execution.

"Warren!"

Execution. His tiny visitor had almost made him forget he was waiting to see his father. Warren spun on his heels and headed for the study.

"Hullo, Father." If he had hoped the brightness of his salutation would lighten his father's mood, he was sorely mistaken.

"Sit," his father said without lifting his head. His elbows rested on the large, carved desk while his hands cradled his head, roughly massaging his temples. Winston Mallory looked worn and defeated, a strange thing for a man known for his composure and levelheadedness in business matters. Warren had no idea what had transpired minutes earlier in this room, but he wished it hadn't happened right before he was to receive discipline.

"Listen, if now isn't a good time—"

"A good time? Is there ever a good time to discover your son has defaced school property?" he said, finally lifting his head to lock eyes with Warren.

So, he had indeed heard from the schoolmaster. "Defaced is a strong word," he said.

"Strong word? I'll give you strong words." Winston Mallory rose and slammed his knuckles onto the desk. "Boarding school!"

Warren winced as if he had been slapped. He wished he had been slapped.

"Father, I'll pay for the damages—"

"You? How will you pay? Have you acquired employment that I am unaware of?"

Warren swallowed. "I have my allowances."

"Not anymore."

Was his father seriously taking away his money? Surely this wasn't happening.

"It was just a harmless prank—"

"It was the final straw."

"But it's my senior year. You can't mean to make me leave now!"

"You've done this to yourself, son," his father said, calming visibly and sitting behind the formidable desk once again. "The superintendent phoned. You've been expelled from Lansing High School."

Warren exhaled slowly and sunk deeper into his chair. Expelled. In all his mischief, through all his disobedience and rebellion over the years, expulsion had never crossed his mind. He had been through one scrape after another, but he had always come out fairly unscathed. How was it possible this close to graduation? Had he really gotten himself so irreversibly ensnared in such a trouble? But even as the thought settled to reality in his mind, the truth of his father's words washed over him. Warren had indeed done this to himself.

He wasn't a bad person. Well, at least he didn't think so. He just had a mischievous streak in him that he never could quite control. He hadn't always been like this. But when his mother died, his father threw himself into work leaving Warren to fill most of his free time on his own. There is no better cure for the sickness of boredom than mischief, and young Warren found himself curing his ailment with this prescription more often than not.

"Where will I go?" Warren asked.

"I've contacted Walthamshire and they have agreed to take you. You leave the beginning of next week."

Warren shuddered inwardly. Although his father always spoke highly of his alma mater, Warren always imagined it the worst of all places on earth. Not only would he spend the remainder of his school days stuffed in a stiff uniform, his mind would be expected to conform to their stiff religious practices as well.

Warren shuffled out of his father's study in a much different mood than when he had entered. He stopped in the middle of the hall, his mind spinning with all the things he needed to do. Having never been away from home for more than a month, he had no idea where to begin preparing. He looked into the drawing room and contemplated stretching out on the settee again to think, but something caught his eye from beneath the throne Grace had just vacated.

"Well, hello there Gertrude." He smiled as he picked up the doll. "I may have a lot to do over the next few days, but you, my little friend, have just made it to the top of the list."

MRS. TRUDY'S SHOP

ansing, Michigan April 1918

"WHERE'D YA GET THAT OUTFIT?"

Anna continued piecing the bodice together of the evening dress. Without looking up, she answered her surly co-worker. "This is the same one I have been working on since Monday, for Miss Leonne's debut at the Gladmer this weekend."

"I meant the one yer wearin'," came the caustic reply.

Anna knew exactly what Irene had meant. The other woman always made it very clear that she disapproved of Anna's choice in clothing, and she had expected no less today. She stole a sideway glance at her mother who was working diligently on the skirt embroidery of an afternoon dress and saw that she would receive no help from her. Dressed in a sensible skirt and armistice blouse, her mother likely agreed that Anna's choice in the cream linen walking suit was a bit too swank for a day spent laboring in the back of a dressmaker's shop.

"It is just another piece I've refashioned from an old one," she finally said with a sigh, hoping Irene would notice her irritation and leave her be.

Fashion had always changed quickly, and luckily for Anna, it had moved in a decidedly slimmer, more slender profile than the flouncier, fabric burdened styles of only a decade ago. Sensibilities brought on by the Great War had seen to that. Had the opposite been true, she would have had a hard time converting her mother's old wardrobe into anything passable as stylish. But, as it was, Anna found it fairly easy to create new pieces from the old, and her mother had an almost inexhaustible supply of beautiful gowns, skirts and day suits for Anna to adjust in her spare time.

"Hmmmph," Irene grunted. "Ridiculous if ya ask me. Wearin' fancy duds like that, puttin' on airs when you ain't no better than the rest of us."

Irene's nasal Michigan accent grated on Anna's nerves. The laziness of her speech, though not as relaxed as the southern transplants that had moved north for work in the auto factories, was still too lethargic to care much about finishing words properly. Although she had lived here most of her life, Anna doubted she would ever grow accustomed to the accent.

"I'm not trying to appear better than anyone," Anna said, weaving her needle back and forth in her usual rhythmic pattern. "But if I like to look nice, and it makes me happy, well, why should anyone else care?"

Her mother had been reluctant at first to allow Anna to tear apart any of her former wardrobe. Anna understood. The clothing was about all that was left of their former lifestyle of wealth and privilege. Taking that away from Elizabeth Gibson was akin to tearing open a scabbed over wound. But Elizabeth had allowed her daughter to choose one dress, and the result was so pleasing to both women that it became a regular practice, filling most evenings with ripped seams and pinned hems scattered about their tiny rented room. It was a slow process, but a process that occupied otherwise empty evenings and, slowly but surely, Anna was creating a small wardrobe for both herself and her mother that would make it very difficult to tell that they were such an impoverished pair.

"All I'm sayin' is that it's a shame wastin' so much time trying to make yourself look so good, an' for what? Roy down at the diner?"

Anna shuddered at the thought of the gruff cook from Jimmy's Café. She certainly had no intention of gaining the attention of that one, or any other man for that matter. Anna had only met one man in her entire life worth fussing over, and she wasn't so certain that he hadn't been a figment of her little girl's imagination. No, she held no fantasies of ensnaring a gentleman with her beauty. She just liked to look nice for herself, and that was all there was to it. It also pleased her to see her mother dressed well. It felt as if, in some small way, Anna was able to give her mother back a portion of the dignity that life had cruelly ripped from her.

"Oh, dear," Mrs. Trudy said as she entered the room in a near panic. None of the seamstresses stopped their work or bothered to acknowledge the shop owner's dramatic entrance. There was much work to accomplish today, and Mrs. Trudy was forever in 'a panic.' "Anna! Miss Leonne has arrived for her fitting…two hours early!"

"It's all right." Anna suppressed the urge to laugh at the shop owner's flushed cheeks and heaving chest. "I just finished piecing the bodice, and the skirt is already all basted together. There wasn't much more I could accomplish before fitting it to her anyway."

"Oh, I'm glad to hear it, glad to hear it, my dear," she said. She continued to enthusiastically fan herself with a lace hand-kerchief. "I will show her to one of the rooms."

Moments later, Anna walked into one of the larger fitting

rooms where Miss Charlotte Leonne waited for her. Besides being an accomplished stage actress and singer, Miss Leonne also fancied herself a fashion icon. In the throngs of a place like New York City, she would probably go unnoticed. But in the Midwest mecca that was Lansing, Michigan, she stood out prominently as the epitome of style. The other seamstresses wanted nothing to do with her. They said it was because she was too picky and demanding, but Anna knew they were intimidated more by who she was than by how she acted. But Anna didn't mind. She had spent the first half of her life surrounded by women far richer than Miss Leonne, and the fact that she was particular about how she wanted her clothing made Anna's job much easier. As long as she listened to her during the first consultation, Anna never had to redo a piece for Miss Leonne. Miss Leonne would give an exhaustive description of what she wanted, often with a picture or a rudimentary sketch, and Anna would fulfill every request. Eventually, as their relationship developed, Anna learned where she could take liberties with design, and this seemed to please Miss Leonne.

"Oh, Anna! I love the train! Whatever made you think to do it that way?"

"I don't know," Anna laughed, pinning the hem of the gown as Miss Leonne admired her reflection in the mirror. "Since French lace is so difficult to come by these days, I wanted to do something else special, something unique for this piece. The fabric reminded me of water, so I thought it would look nice cascading from the shoulders like that. Sometimes the fabric just tells me what it would like to do, I guess."

The woman laughed. "Well, I'm certainly glad it did! My idea would have made for a pretty version, but this...*this* gown will be the talk of the papers for a week!"

Anna smiled as she stuffed half a dozen pins between her teeth. Her mother always chastised her for such an unladylike act, but kneeling on the floor of a dress shop for the better part of her day didn't lend itself to ladylikeness either.

"I know that it is in poor taste to wear colorful clothing during the day, now that we are at war, but I'm so glad that rule is lifted for evening wear, aren't you?" Miss Leonne twirled on the little platform, smiling at her own reflection in the blue evening gown. "You know, you could get triple what I pay Trudy for this in New York, or even Detroit. You should really consider going out on your own. I know of quite a few design houses that would give anything for a talent like yourself."

To her credit, Miss Leonne had never treated Anna as anything but an equal. She saw Anna as an artist, not unlike herself, and often encouraged Anna to pursue a career in design. As much as Anna appreciated the compliment, her life did not lend itself to the pursuit of idyllic dreams or fantasies. Although she and her mother both worked at the shop, the elder Gibson woman never acquired any expertise beyond embroidery, a talent in which all English women of noble birth were trained. But fashion was demanding less and less embroidery these days, making her mother's skills less in demand. Without Anna's pay as a seamstress, her mother would not be able to live.

Anna pinned the last of the dress's hem and rose, smoothing out the wrinkles of her linen suit. Miss Leonne turned from the mirror and looked at Anna from head to toe.

"Or maybe they couldn't afford you," she said with a grin. "That suit, it's beautiful. Did you design it yourself?"

Anna dropped her gaze. Maybe this outfit was a bit too extravagant for her line of work. "Yes, in a manner of speaking."

"You must do very well to afford fine linen like that. I want one," she said, hands on her hips. "How much?"

"I – I'm not certain," Anna said, running her hands down the front of the jacket. Miss Leonne was correct. This was very fine linen. Anna wasn't sure if Mrs. Trudy had anything like it in her supply. She would likely have to order it, but with the war going on in France, Anna wasn't certain from where. "I'm sure if you speak with Mrs. Trudy–"

"No," Miss Leonne whispered, "I'll not buy it from Mrs. Trudy. I want you to make it for me on your own. I want to buy it from you."

"Oh, but I couldn't," Anna whispered back. "If Mrs. Trudy found out…"

Charlotte Leonne stepped off the platform and stood close to Anna and placed her hands on Anna's shoulders. "Then she mustn't find out," she said quietly. "Anna, I wouldn't be where I am today if someone hadn't taken a risk on me and invested in my life. I might still be some two-bit actress cleaning hotel rooms to pay my rent if they hadn't. That's what I want to do for you. I want to invest in your future, Anna. I want you to make me a beautiful suit like that. One that when others see it, they know for certain that I didn't purchase it off the rack at Knapp's or Arbaugh's. So when asked, I can proudly say, 'Oh this? Why, this is an Anna Gibson original.' Then see how long before you are the hottest designer this side of Lake Erie!"

She wasn't certain what to say, but she knew that it could mean her job if Mrs. Trudy overheard their conversation. As if sensing her discomfort, Miss Leonne gave her a wink and took a step back.

"We'll discuss it further when you deliver my dress to the Gladmer. Can you have it to me by tomorrow afternoon?" She turned her back so Anna could assist her with removing the dress.

"Of course," Anna answered. She had never delivered a dress before, but since the little shop was located on the outskirts of Lansing's theater district, she could see no reason not to fulfill the request. Mrs. Trudy would not object, and Anna had never seen the inside of the Gladmer theater. It would be a pleasant diversion, she was certain.

"Terrific," Miss Leonne settled into her own afternoon dress, another piece of Anna's work. She cinched her Dorothy bag and slung it on her wrist before sweeping towards the door. She stopped and turned just as she touched the doorknob. "Oh, I almost forgot! I've procured two tickets for you and a guest for opening night. I'll have them for you when you drop off my dress." With that, she was gone before Anna had a chance to object.

Two tickets to an opening night at the Gladmer? Anna had been to a couple of theaters, of which Lansing had several, but only on the nights they played a moving picture show. She had never been to a play with real actors and an orchestra. She remembered as a child watching her mother ready herself for the theater and thinking it must be the most elegant of all places on earth. And now, she had an opportunity to go herself. But as exciting as the prospect was, the thought actually nauseated Anna. How could she attend such an elegant event? In all of her time spent sewing and refashioning a new wardrobe, it had never once occurred to her to rework an evening gown. And Saturday was only three days away.

～

"NONSENSE," her mother chided, picking up a well-worn copy of *Nicholas Nickleby*. "You must go. There simply is no excuse good enough to miss an opportunity like this."

"No excuse? How about 'I have nothing to wear'?"

"Rubbish. You are surrounded by half a dozen gowns, Anna. Just choose one and work your magic. You have three nights. You've accomplished far more in less time than that."

"Yes, three nights, but two gowns, Mother. You will need an appropriate dress as well."

"Me? Oh, Anna, surely you would rather attend with one of your friends. Esther, perhaps?"

"No, I want to go with you. Besides, I'm not certain Esther's father would let her attend. I don't believe he sees the theater as a completely wholesome activity for young women."

"I hadn't thought about that." Her mother dropped the book to her lap. "But I've been to the theater many times. Are you certain there isn't someone else you'd rather accompany you?"

Anna rolled her eyes. Her mother knew as well as Anna did that, besides Esther, none of the women Anna associated with would have the appropriate attire for an evening at the theater just hanging in her closet waiting for an invitation. "No, Mother. No one besides you."

"Well, then I will just have to wear one of my gowns as is. It is more important that a young woman be fitted in the current fashion. An elderly widow like myself will do quite nicely in any of those dresses just as they are."

At forty-two, Elizabeth Gibson was anything but elderly. She had married young, a necessity for the only daughter of a penniless English earl, and had given birth to her only child by the time she turned twenty. As an adult now, Anna could see that her parents' marriage had been one of convenience, but they were both kind people that adored their daughter, and life together had been a comfortable coexistence that created a safe haven for little Anna. But that comfort was destroyed when her father passed away. The middle son of a Pennsylvania lumber tycoon, Henry Gibson had the idea to uproot his small family and relocate to Michigan to try his hand at the automobile industry. He invested in a small wheel making company and moved Anna and her mother into a rented townhouse until a suitable home could be built. It was his dream to make a name for himself, apart from his father, but that dream ended when, by a sad twist of fate, her father was killed in an automobile accident on his way to Detroit to negotiate the transportation of materials.

Losing one's spouse and father would have been enough to devastate Elizabeth and young Anna, but their troubles were only made worse when it was discovered that Henry Gibson died without a will. With no will, Elizabeth Gibson had no rights. Any shares in his father's lumber business that belonged to Henry reverted back to the elder Mr. Gibson. Henry's father had never approved of his marriage to the English born Elizabeth. Still sore about Great Britain's involvement with the confederate states during the civil war, Thomas Gibson felt a certain vindication cutting Elizabeth and her daughter off from the profits of his company. And since Elizabeth had no intentions of begging, she accepted the shunning with quiet dignity.

Elizabeth and Anna lived for a time on the money Henry had left in the bank, but a large portion of his wealth had been invested in the wheel company. Since the lack of a will also meant the wheel company had no obligation to repay the widow of the investor, Elizabeth and Anna quickly found themselves in dire straits. When the money ran out, Elizabeth began selling off the few valuables they had brought with them to Michigan. When that supply was exhausted, Elizabeth found a small room above a bookstore to rent.

Thus, Elizabeth, former daughter of an earl and wife of a tycoon, found herself using the only talent she had, embroidery, to support herself and her young daughter. It was there, in the back of that tiny shop, that Anna would sit at her mother's feet, passing the time between learning the art of embroidery and learning to sew from the other women in the shop. The dressmakers would slip her the discarded scraps of fabric from their work and she would diligently practice the different stitches they taught her. She was a quick study, and was soon making dresses for her china doll, another of the few relics left from their former life.

Anna watched her mother who had returned to her novel. She had made so many sacrifices for the two of them. When other women would have cursed God or blamed the world for her misfortunes, Elizabeth had turned her mourning into hard work, never stopping in her praise to the Creator for his love and mercy. They weren't rich financially, but they lived a comfortable life that exemplified the merits of hard work and faith. For that example, Anna was so very grateful. She smiled. She would finish her dress, and one for her mother, by Saturday, even if it meant no sleep for the next few days. Her mother deserved this night out, and Anna was going to make certain she got it.

2

THE GLADMER

"Oh, Anna! It's divine!" her mother beamed, enraptured by her own reflection in the mirror.

"Do you like it? Truly?"

Her mother turned from the mirror and grasped her daughter's hands.

"So much, my dear. God has given you a great gift."

"I feared you would be upset...that the dress I chose would upset you."

Of all of Elizabeth's wardrobe, her finest gowns had always seemed untouchable to Anna, not because of their monetary value, but because of their sentimental sensibilities. When Henry Gibson passed away, rather than purchase a new collection of frocks for mourning, Elizabeth Gibson had decided to dip some of her wardrobe instead, and rather than choosing the least of her gowns and dresses, she chose the finest. Thus, when it came time to make her mother's gown, Anna found herself in a quandary...make a dress out of something ordinary or create a dress worthy of her mother at the risk of reminding her mother of sadder times. Anna chose the latter. Seeing her mother's breathtaking appearance, she did not regret her decision.

19

Elizabeth turned back to the mirror. "Oh, no, darling. I love it. You have taken something that once symbolized sadness and have brought me joy. I'm just so amazed at your cleverness. How did you come to the conclusion that these two dresses should merge?"

Anna fingered the black beadwork that she had cut from the mourning dress. "It came to me when I was sorting through your gowns. I had thrown the ivory one across the bed, and when I tossed the black dress there as well, the sheer overlay of the skirt looked gorgeous against the cream silk. But it wasn't until I was cutting the black dress apart that I was inspired to lay the beadwork like feathers. And since hats aren't acceptable for the theater–"

"Thank goodness, because where would we ever find a hat to match this dress!"

Anna laughed. "I'm not certain. But a black headband and feather woven through your hair…now that is the perfect accessory for you tonight!"

"I adore it." Her mother smiled at her reflection in the mirror. "And you are a vision of which even Madame Gerber would be envious!"

"Is it that obvious?" Anna laughed. "I have been studying the designs from Callot Soeurs."

Anna had chosen a pale pink dress for herself. She had been inspired by a design she had seen in a Callot Soeurs advertisement in the New York Times. However, rather than the heavy, Orientalists textiles and lavish embroidery that were signature elements of the famous French design house, she opted for a lightweight chiffon to cascade down the back of her dress like a fabric waterfall. With the excess fabric pieces, she crafted a wide band to tie around her head.

"Oh, no, dear," her mother said as Anna started to tie the fabric in place. "I have something far more beautiful."

Elizabeth Gibson reached under their bed and pulled out an old, weathered box. She lifted the lid and pulled out a smaller box buried beneath a pile of old letters. Inside the small box was the most beautiful brooch Anna had ever seen.

"Oh, my," Anna said, delicately tracing the pinkish gems that circled the jewel. "I thought you sold all the jewelry that Father gave you?"

"Your father didn't buy me this piece. A friend of the family did."

"Are those diamonds?"

"Austrian crystals. It's always been a favorite of mine, but I guess I held on to it…well, for sentimental reasons, I suppose. Do you see how the color changes in the light?"

"It changes from blue to pink!"

"It is perfect with your dress," Elizabeth said, moving to stand behind Anna. "But I think you should wear it in your hair."

She carefully pinned the brooch at the back of Anna's hair. "There. Now you are ready for the theater."

IT WAS a short walk to the Gladmer from their tiny apartment. Anna had considered hiring a cab, but had dismissed the idea. It would be absurd to pay for a vehicle to drive them the two blocks that separated their home from the theater. Besides, if they timed it right, the crowds would be so great when they arrived that no one would notice whether they arrived by motor or foot.

Anna had been correct in her prediction of the crowd. When they arrived at the Gladmer, lines of theater goers thronged around the entrance, some trying their best to enter in a timely manner, while others seemed quite content to languish their time outside with a cigarette. As Anna and her mother passed through the haze of one gathering of smokers, Anna was overcome with a coughing fit. The group just stared at her as if she had somehow interrupted their pleasant evening. She would never understand the fascination some people had with the nasty smelling sticks.

Being under the scrutiny of the passing group, if even for a moment, made Anna uncomfortable. Her hand rose to her neck and her fingers self-consciously traced an invisible line, naked compared to the other women's heavily bejeweled throats. Maybe coming to the theater was not a wise decision. What if, despite her best efforts to look the part of a privileged woman who often frequented the theater, she looked like nothing more than an urchin lost in her wanderings? What if everyone could see through her ruse? Would they begin whispering to each other, asking who is this unfortunate girl trying to act like us?

Anna looked at her mother out of the corner of her eye. She had not only attended the theater on several occasions, she had spent most of her life surrounded by people like those around them now. Anna need only look to her for clues on how she should be behaving. But when she looked at her, she didn't find the calm, poised woman she expected to see. Her mother seemed agitated. Although her eyes remained focused ahead, her hands nervously picked at the handle of her purse and absentmindedly adjusted the seams of her white gloves. She eventually stopped this fidgeting, but within seconds, her delicate fingers began tapping the clip on her bag.

"Mother, is everything alright?" Anna asked, reaching for her hand and giving it a squeeze.

Her mother squeezed back. "Yes, dear. I'm just a little excited."

Anna wasn't convinced, but it was their turn to pass into the theater. Once inside, they followed the crowd through the foyer toward doors that she assumed led to the auditorium. When it was their turn, Anna tried to keep her hands steady as she handed their tickets to the young man at the auditorium doors. He looked at their tickets and handed them back to her.

"You don't belong here."

Anna wobbled over shaky knees. Had her ruse failed?

The usher frowned at her. "To your right, miss," he said, taking the tickets from the couple behind her and continuing on to the next.

"I beg your pardon?" Anna's heart thudded against her breastbone.

The usher nodded toward his left without looking up. "Box J. To your right, miss."

Anna didn't understand, but she felt a tug at her elbow from her mother. They moved out of the flow, away from the pressing crowd.

"Let me see our tickets, dear," her mother said, taking them from Anna. "Oh, I see. This way." She guided them to the side of the foyer where a much smaller entrance was attended by two serious looking ushers. Neither of them spoke when Elizabeth handed one of them the tickets. He only nodded, removed the velvet roping, and led the two women up a narrow passageway.

Anna hadn't expected center orchestra seats, but she didn't expect terrible seating either. Miss Leonne was the star of the show, for goodness sake. But the farther up they went, the more convinced she became that their seats were located on the roof with a view of the back alley.

When at last the usher stopped, he pulled back a tall, dark drapery, allowing Anna and her mother to enter a small, rounded balcony with seating for only six. It wasn't square, but Anna knew without a doubt they were seated in an opera box.

"Mother," Anna whispered. "These are good seats, are they not?"

"They are splendid seats," her mother smiled. "The most splendid in the entire house."

Anna marveled at their fortune. She would make sure to thank Miss Leonne with a little something special on her next commissioned piece.

Two more seats were quickly filled with a pleasant looking elderly couple. The lights dimmed, making introductions impossible for now, but Anna smiled when she saw out of the corner of her eye the gentleman's gnarled fingers reach over and grasp his wife's hand. Anna reached for her mother's hand and gave it a squeeze.

"I'm fine now." She smiled at Anna. "It's about to begin."

The lights continued to dim until the entire auditorium was black. Anna's heart pounded so hard, she wondered if the other members of their small box could hear it beat as loudly as she could. Just when she thought she could no longer stand the anticipation, the large, black drapery hiding the stage from their view swung open.

It was spectacular. Anna was swept away with the story and the music. Oh, the music! So many talented performers were cast in this production, but none could hold a candle to Miss Charlotte Leonne. Her angelic soprano gave Anna goosebumps. During one of the more emotional love songs, Anna pulled her attention away from the stage to observe the audience. Although it was impossible to see the faces of those seated in the back balcony, the stage lights illuminated the first third of the floor seating, which gave Anna many profiles to watch. Some women dabbed their eyes with lace handkerchiefs, while others blinked rapidly in an attempt to dry away the moisture before it collected into droplets. Anna had to stifle a giggle when she saw one portly, balding gentleman use his coat sleeve to wipe the tears that fell with abandon down his cheeks.

Anna's gaze traveled from the floor seats up the wall to the box seating opposite them. The angle of their seating gave her a much better view of their emotions and Anna took her time observing each one. Her gaze passed over each face, male and female, and she wondered at the power Miss Leonne's voice had over people's emotions. Tenderness, fear, shock, excitement, and more crossed the faces she scanned. Her eyes arrived to the last box, and she froze. In the box directly across from them, there was one gentleman not engrossed in the play. He was watching Anna.

Anna gasped and dropped her gaze. She had no idea if it

was rude to watch other people during a performance or not, but if so, then she had just been very rude indeed. She knew she should keep her eyes on the stage, but she couldn't help looking up at the man again. He was still staring, but now Anna wasn't certain that he was staring at her. She glanced at her mother and noticed that her fingers had begun tapping her handbag again. She looked back at the man. He was clearly oblivious to Anna. She leaned in slightly to her mother and whispered, "I think you have an admirer."

"I know," her mother whispered back, never taking her eyes off the stage.

Anna straightened in her seat and watched the man. It was difficult to tell, but he appeared to be tall. His hair was dark, except where time had begun to lighten it at the temples and throughout his facial hair, which was well groomed and trimmed to a point.

"He's quite handsome," Anna whispered.

"Pay attention to the play, Anna."

Her mother's discomfort was entertaining to Anna. With a woman as beautiful as Elizabeth Gibson, it was not unusual for her to draw the attention of men. But Anna had never seen her mother even notice these men, let alone be unsettled by their attentions. And with this gentleman so entirely engrossed with Elizabeth, Anna took the opportunity to observe him very thoroughly.

"He looks to be about your age…"

"Stop it."

"Maybe a little older, but not enough to be bothersome."

"Stop staring at him. It is abundantly rude."

"Well, then I suppose he is being rude first. I'm just returning the favor."

"You're going to get caught."

"By whom?" she snickered. "He isn't about to take his eyes off of you just to catch me looking!"

"He isn't the only person in the theater."

"Tell him that! I think he has forgotten that the two of you aren't alone in here!"

Anna watched the muscle of her mother's jaw clench and she knew her mother was not going to engage in this banter any longer. She could not suppress the smile this caused, and she looked one last time to see if the man had given up on gaining her mother's attention. He had not, and his unguarded appreciation for her mother made Anna smile even wider. She sighed and was about to return her attention to the action of the play, when she noticed something she hadn't before. A movement behind the staring gentleman caught her eye. In the darker recess of the box, sitting behind her mother's admirer, sat another gentleman, and he was looking directly at Anna.

In a panic, Anna turned back to the play and held her breath. Had that really just happened? Had she just been caught staring? Oh, why didn't she listen to her mother's pleas?

Anna tried to focus on the scene below, but she could not erase the image of the staring eyes. Maybe she was wrong. Maybe she was mistaken like she had been with the first gentleman. Maybe this one was looking at her mother as well, or maybe the older woman beside her. Anna had to admit the latter was unlikely, but she was grasping for any explanation other than what she feared. She knew she shouldn't, but she couldn't stop herself from looking once more, praying she had been wrong. But when she looked again, the evidence was there, staring back at her, and this time it was accompanied by a large, confident smile.

The rest of the scene was pure torture for Anna. She had lost complete grasp of what was happening in the play, but she didn't dare take her eyes off the stage. She concentrated so hard on the actors, that when her eyes began to burn, she realized she hadn't blinked in ages. When the curtain finally fell, the darkness of the theater brought temporary relief to Anna's agony. But as the house lights began to brighten, she realized she would be much more exposed.

"Would you ladies care to join us for some fresh air?" the elderly gentleman sharing their box asked.

"Yes!" Anna exclaimed, turning to her mother. "That is, if you are up to it, Mother."

"Air sounds lovely," her mother smiled.

As Anna rose from her seat, her eyes betrayed her by stealing a glance at the opposite box. The staring eyes were no longer there. Anna's relief gave way to fear. What if she ran into the man in the foyer or outside the theater. What would she say? How would she explain herself?

"Actually, if you don't mind, I think I'll stay." She sat back down. Without a ticket, the man could not possibly gain access to this side of the theater. He may be able to see her, but he would not be able to confront her. "I'd love to spend some time admiring the beautiful architecture."

"The Gladmer is quite a beautiful sight," the gentleman agreed. "We'll bring you some punch."

When they had gone, Anna nervously looked about the room, trying to appear as nonchalant as possible. Her eyes swept across the theater, barely stopping at the box opposite her, and, to her relief, it was completely empty. Even her mother's admirer had taken the opportunity to stretch his legs.

Anna finally relaxed and took in the beauty the Gladmer offered. The sculpted architecture, with its carved relief friezes, arched over not only the grand stage, but each of the six opera boxes opposite where she sat. Although it was difficult to know for sure, she assumed her side of the theater was a mirror image of what she was looking at...three on top of three curved boxes flanked by Grecian inspired columns. It was hard to tell in the still somewhat dim lighting, but the murals above the stage and boxes appeared to be a floral motif. This surprised Anna. With all of the carvings and cherubim statues, she would have expected something more Renaissance, like a depiction of Michaelangelo's *The Creation of Adam* or something of the like.

"Do you like what you see?" said a male voice from behind her.

Anna didn't turn around. She knew without a doubt that it was the man from across the theater. She didn't know how he had accomplished it, but he had found his way into her box.

She did not respond. She continued admiring the carved architectural pieces, or at least attempted to, praying that the man would take the hint and leave her alone. When she saw the pinstripes of his pants slip into the seat beside her, she knew he had not.

"Do you like what you see?" he repeated softly. He leaned scandalously close and his warm breath brushed Anna's ear like a hot summer breeze.

"Yes," she answered stiffly. She concentrated on slowing her breath which had quickened with the man's arrival. "The reliefs are quite stunning."

"Hmmmm…yes, I find the beauty off the stage this evening very distracting as well."

Could he hear her heart thumping in her throat? She swallowed quickly.

"I didn't say the architecture was distracting…"

"Neither did I."

Anna clenched her fists. Her breath again raced at the speed of her heartbeat, but she had no idea how to control it. If only her mother would return and save her from this situation. How long had she been gone? Surely, she would return soon.

"Actually, I find the play quite captivating," Anna lied, trying to return the conversation to safer ground.

"Do you now? What did you think of the main character's reaction to the murder?"

There had been a murder? Anna blinked a few times, trying desperately to piece together the parts of the play she had watched. She hadn't ignored the entire production, but sitting here with this man so close and speaking so softly, she could barely remember her own name, let alone anything about the silly play.

As she sat struggling for her next words, the gentleman's arm brushed her bare shoulder as it slide across the back of her seat. He leaned even closer to her ear. "You are very beautiful," he whispered.

"You are being presumptuous, sir!"

"You are being elusive, miss." He withdrew slightly.

"I am just trying to enjoy the view."

"So am I," he laughed. "Come, now. Can't we just give up this game and admit what we were both looking at...each other."

He thought she was looking at him. She wasn't certain if this were better or more horrifying.

"I wasn't looking at you," she insisted.

"You were either looking at me or the old man in front of me. I suppose it could have been him." He crossed his arms across his chest and leaned back in the chair. "But if that is the truth, then I will be sorely disappointed...and more than slightly confused. He is quite a bit too old for you, don't you think?"

Anna shuddered inwardly. She had never felt more trapped. Again, she wished she had listened to her mother.

"I wasn't looking at either of you. As I said before, I was admiring the architectural sculpture."

The man leaned forward and rested his elbows on his knees. It was a very relaxed posture to assume in public, Anna thought, but it afforded her the opportunity to get somewhat of a look at her inquisitor without turning her head. His evening suit jacket stretched across strong, wide shoulders, making it appear a size too small, she thought. She couldn't see his face, really, but she noticed how neatly his chestnut hair was trimmed.

"Yes, yes I see," he said in mock agreement. "That large, plain, black drapery behind my seat is rather interesting to look at. No wonder you couldn't take your eyes from it."

Anna ignored that remark and turned her head away from

the man. He leaned back in the seat once again. She felt him touch a strand of hair that had come loose from her Pompadour.

"It's hard to tell in this lighting, but if I were to guess, I'd say it is amber."

"Do you make a habit of touching women's hair without their permission?" she said coolly. When would this man take the hint and leave.

He dropped his hand and sighed. "Why won't you admit that you were looking at me. Aren't you a modern woman like every other girl out there."

"Actually, I am quite the Gibson Girl," Anna said, enjoying the pun her name allowed.

The man snickered. "You are even prettier when you smirk."

"Then I will be truly breathtaking when you finally take your leave of me, because then you will see my brightest smile yet."

He threw his head back in a hearty laugh. "Well, a man can endure only so much rejection—"

"And yet you are still here."

"So, I will depart. But fear not, beautiful maiden. You have convinced me that you were not staring at me—"

"I am happy to hear that."

"And I will be certain to let the old man know that it is he, not I, that has drawn the attention of the captivating, amber-haired beauty."

Anna's head snapped toward the man. "You would not —" she began, but the words stuck in her throat.

His hazel eyes crinkled in the corners as a smile slowly slid across his face. "Wouldn't I?" said Warren Mallory.

3

WARREN

*S*he couldn't believe what she was seeing. He couldn't be real, could he? She had dreamed of him so many times, she must be dreaming now. Her mind told her to reach out and touch him, to test the palpability of this manifestation of her imagination, but she couldn't get her body to cooperate. She couldn't do anything but stare, open-mouthed and wide-eyed at him.

His crooked smile widened and he leaned closer. He spoke to her so softly, the hair on the back of her neck stood on end. "With amber eyes to match," he said.

It was really him. Sitting next to her, like an apparition from her past, was Warren. He had grown older, more mature, but she would have recognized him anywhere. He was even more handsome than she remembered, and he was smiling at her, talking to her, calling her beautiful. Did he recognize her? Is that why he was being so bold? It had been thirteen years. Surely he didn't...

The lights flickered, signaling the show was about to begin again.

"Meet me out front after the end of the play. Don't say no," he whispered.

She couldn't say no. She couldn't say anything.

"I'll be waiting on the corner of Ionia and Washington. You'll be there?"

She felt her head nodding. Warren kissed her hand, in the same gallant way he had the last time she saw him all those years ago, and slipped through the curtain of her box. Anna wasn't certain how long she sat staring at the dark drapes, but it wasn't until the elderly couple returned through the same curtain that her daze ended. She turned in her seat to find Warren smiling at her from across the theater. It hadn't been a dream. It was real. Warren was real. And he was smiling at her.

"Here dear," the elderly woman said. "You must have dropped this," she said, placing a small box wrapped in almond-colored paper into her hand.

"I'm sorry, but it isn't mine," Anna protested.

"Well, it isn't mine, and I'm certain it wasn't here when we left. You are the only other person it could possibly belong to."

Warren. He must have dropped it.

"Thank you very much," Anna said, slipping the tiny package into her purse. She would return it to him when she saw him after the performance.

The auditorium grew dark again as the curtains slowly slid open. Anna's mother quietly slipped into her seat as the first line of the act was recited.

"I have something very exciting to tell you," Anna whispered.

"It will have to wait."

Anna settled back into her seat, certain that she would explode from the anticipation of it all. She tried her best to concentrate on the play, but no matter how hard she attempted to focus on the actors, all she saw were Warren's hazel eyes staring back at her. It didn't help that his real eyes remained on her for the remainder of the play. Every time she glanced his way, she caught him staring at her, not the least bit embarrassed at being caught.

After what seemed a torturous eternity, final curtain fell, ending the play. The house erupted in applause, and Anna's excitement grew as the moment was almost here when she would finally see Warren again. All she needed to do was suffer through the curtain call, and she could leave.

"Come, Anna. Quickly," her mother whispered frantically in the dark, grabbing Anna by the wrist. In shock, Anna allowed herself to be hauled into the dimly lit passageway before stopping her mother.

"What are you doing?" she asked, wrenching herself free from her mother's grasp.

"Please, Anna. Please don't ask questions. I need to leave – now."

Anna had never seen her mother so desperate before and it broke her heart. She nodded and followed quickly behind. They rushed down the corridor toward the front entrance. When they crossed the intersection of Washington and Ionia, Anna couldn't stop the tears from spilling down her flushed cheeks. Only moments ago, her life had taken on new meaning, a renewed hope, and now, for reasons unknown to her, that future was destroyed. She was missing her opportunity to reconnect with Warren... and she had no idea why.

ONCE INSIDE THEIR APARTMENT, Anna collapsed into the faded wing chair. The rush of their race home had dried the tears from her cheeks and cooled her emotions. In fact, Anna wasn't certain what, if anything, she was feeling right now. But as she sat watching her mother, back turned to Anna, casually removing her gloves and readying for bed, she felt an emotion rising that she had never felt toward her before. Anger.

"I believe I deserve an explanation." Anna's clenched fists shook at her side.

Her mother did not turn. She removed her earrings.

"Mother! I demand you explain yourself."

Elizabeth placed her hands on the dresser and dropped her head. She still said nothing.

The back of her throat burned as bile rose to the top. She stood, clenching her fists at her side. How dare her mother ruin her evening, then ignore her pleas for answers? Anna took a deep breath.

But, something stopped her. It was the slightest of movements, but it was there. Her mother's shoulders were shaking. Anna hadn't seen her mother cry since her father's death. Not when Grandfather Gibson cut them off, not when the creditors started coming around, not when they were forced to move from their home, not when she took employment in the dress shop. The realization instantly doused Anna's mounting anger and she rushed to her mother's side.

"What has happened? Are you hurt?" She turned her mother toward her and searched her face. "I'm so sorry I yelled. Please don't cry." Anna led her to the settee that, along with the faded wingback, a small table and chairs and their bed, made up the furnishings of their home. She handed her mother a handkerchief and wrapped her arms around her shoulders while her mother wiped her tears.

"I'm so sorry, darling, truly I am," Elizabeth said between sobs. "I should have known this evening would end in disaster. The past is not ours to revive. 'Not that I speak in respect of want: for I have learned, in whatsoever state I am, therewith to be content.'"

"Philippians four," Anna whispered against her mother's shoulder. "I don't understand. You aren't making any sense."

"Contentment, Anna. We should be content with where God has us."

Anna lifted her head. "I am, we are, Mother. We are content with our little life."

"Are we? Then why did we go to the theater tonight? We no longer live in that world. What did we really think we would accomplish with a taste of our former life?"

Anna hadn't considered that. "I—I only hoped for an evening enjoying a play."

"And what next? Would you want more dresses refashioned so you could attend more social events? Where exactly would you go next? No ball invitations are likely to arrive, Anna. But now that you've had a taste of that life, can you be content with the life God has given us?"

Anna pondered her mother's words. "Mother, you had more than one evening of that life. That was your entire life, but you are content with God's will now. Why wouldn't I be content?"

"Maybe that's the problem, Anna. Maybe I'm not as content as I thought. I thought I had moved on. I thought I had forgiven. I thought I could dip my toe into the water and come back dry, but all tonight has shown me is what we have lost. What you have lost."

"Me?"

"Yes. You should be going to the theater. You should be going to dinner parties and balls and social gatherings and meeting people your age. That would have been your life. Should have been your life. You deserved a gentile upbringing, an introduction to society. You should be choosing a suitor now, not which brocade to pair with what silk."

A suitor. Anna thought again of Warren. She blinked rapidly, willing the wetness that had surfaced there to dry.

"I—I could still meet someone."

"Who? Do you think a man of means is looking for a spouse amongst our kind? No, my dear. The men of that world can't be bothered with women like us."

Anna stroked her mother's arm. "Something has happened

that you aren't telling me. I've never heard you speak so negatively."

"No, you are right. Something did indeed happen tonight. I saw someone I never thought I would see again."

"An old friend?"

"No. Well, yes, I suppose. It's complicated. At one time, yes, I would say I considered him a friend. But after your father's death, he showed himself to be an enemy."

Enemy? She had never heard her mother use such a harsh word to describe another person. "Is he the reason we had to leave in such a hurry?"

Her mother nodded, tears once again spilling down her cheeks. "I thought I had forgiven. I hadn't thought about it in years. But when I saw him tonight and realized we may run into each other, I couldn't breathe. I couldn't stomach the thought of speaking to that traitor."

"Forgiven? Traitor? Who was this man, mother? What has he done?"

Anna watched Elizabeth dab her eyes, then look up, amber eyes locking with amber eyes.

"He is the owner of The Lansing Wheel company."

THE CAR PULLED to a stop and three upset men climbed the front stairs of the Mallory Mansion, each lost in his own thoughts. Not until Warren and George accidentally collided did any of them remember they weren't alone.

"Watch where you're going," George said, pushing his brother.

Warren laughed. "What makes you think that was an accident, little brother?"

"You're a regular Slim Summerville," George said. He eyed his brother suspiciously. "Are you pulling another prank on me, Warren?"

"Prank? What on Earth are you talking about?"

"Never mind." George turned and stormed up the stairs. He stopped halfway and turned. "So help me, if you did this, it isn't funny. The evening was ruined. It's unforgivable," he fumed before making his final exit.

"What's he got stuck up his fundament?" Warren asked in his father's direction.

"Must you speak so coarsely?" his father said.

"I find fundament to be one of the more polite words for that part of the human anatomy," Warren laughed.

"Enough!" Winston Mallory threw his gloves on the entry table. "I don't have the patience for your foolishness. Not tonight."

Warren watched in confusion as his normally placid father stomped up the stairs, slamming his top hat against the newel post at the top.

"Father?"

Winston sighed. "Listen, Warren, just because you had a pleasant evening doesn't mean the rest of us enjoyed the theater." Then, without another word, he disappeared into the darkness of the upstairs hall.

"You haven't any idea," Warren muttered, turning away from the stairs and entering the drawing room. He threw his jacket across the mauve wingback chair and ripped off his necktie. He fell onto the settee and kicked his leg across the arm. Folding his arms behind his head, he looked at the ceiling. It was too dark to count the cracks he knew to be there, but he was too awake to close his eyes. Besides, each time he tried, amber eyes mocked him.

Why was he so upset? So a woman stood him up. What did he expect? Did he think she was as enraptured with him as he had been with her? Of course, that was impossible. No one could be as captivated with another human being as he was with the amber haired beauty.

Maybe it was something he had said, or how he had said it.

It had been so long since he had seriously been interested in a woman, it's no wonder he blundered the exchange. It had gotten so tiresome, all the debutante hopefuls more interested in Warren's wallet than his heart, more focused on the pursuit of an engagement ring than the pursuit of the will of God, that he had given up any hope of finding a woman to share his life with.

But tonight, when he first spotted her across the room, his heart had actually raced. He wondered about her. Who was she? Where was she from? Then, when she looked at him, smiled at him, the rest of the room faded away and he was left with one singular thought – he had to meet her.

Bribing the usher had been the easy part of the mission. Getting the mysterious beauty to warm up to him had been the real difficulty. Oh, but when she finally did, there was no mistaking the connection between them. She felt it as well, or at least he had thought she had felt it. But then why didn't she meet him?

Maybe it was God's way of keeping him from walking outside of His will. God's will. The driving force behind all of Warren's life decisions. Just because this woman was beautiful enough to fascinate him doesn't mean she is the woman God had created for him. But now, Warren will never know. Even though he already had every line of her beautiful face etched in his mind, he didn't know her name.

A noise in the darkness startled him and Warren sat up. He could make out the silhouette of a man moving across the drawing room. He was placing something on the table next to the settee.

"I thought you might like some chamomile tea before retiring," the butler said.

"Chamomile?"

"It relaxes the nerves. I sent some to your father and brother as well."

Warren wasn't thirsty, but he accepted the hot beverage

anyway. He stretched out his long legs and looked up at the shadowy figure.

"Do you see and hear everything that happens in this house?" Warren asked.

"Do you really want to know the answer to that question?" Jameson said. "This arrived for you after you left for the evening."

The soft glow of street lights flowing through the front window of the house illuminated what appeared to be an envelope of some sort. "What is it?" he asked, reaching for it.

"It is sealed, but it appears to be another note from Miss Perry."

Warren smiled. "Thank you, Mr. Jameson. I'll read it in my room."

4

SAVING THE PRINCE

"*W*arren? The man-of-your-dreams Warren? He was there?"

Anna nodded.

"And you spoke with him?"

Anna nodded again.

"What did he say?"

"He asked me to meet him outside after the play."

"And you said no, of course."

Anna smiled at her friend across the table. Esther thought more like Anna's mother than Anna did. Of course Esther would see the impropriety of agreeing to meet a man you just met on the street.

"But, it was Warren," Anna said coyly.

Esther's jaw dropped. "You said yes?"

"Does nodding qualify as agreement?"

"Anna!" Esther said, slamming her half-empty cherry phosphate onto the table. "What happened? My word, I can't believe your mother agreed!"

"She didn't. In fact, she insisted we leave before the final curtain call."

"Wait, you left him standing all alone?" This time it was Phoebe, Esther's younger sister, that spoke. She had been unusually quiet throughout their lunch, but something about abandoning a handsome man on a street corner awoke her to the conversation. "Well, that's not very romantic."

"Romantic? That's a hoot, coming from the one who has sworn off all men!" Esther laughed.

"I haven't sworn them off, just the ones that don't meet a certain standard."

"I'm not certain our Lord Jesus would meet your standards, dear sister."

Anna watched her two dearest friends bicker like the sisters they were. It was a rare occasion to have lunch with both of them these days, with Phoebe off studying at Bible College. She was glad that they had been able to meet for lunch before Phoebe's Easter break ended, even if it did mean she would be getting twice the chastisement for her actions. But they were forgetting Anna's predicament.

"Excuse me," Anna interrupted, "but this is about me, remember?"

"Of course." Esther turned back to Anna. "When will you see him again?"

"Probably never," Anna sighed.

"Never!" Esther cried. "I realize I shuddered at the thought of you meeting him on a poorly lit street corner in the middle of the night, but there must be an alternative somewhere between scandalous liaison and never!"

Anna shrugged her shoulders. "I missed my opportunity. It's too late."

"It can't be too late. This is Warren! Warren who you planned to marry as a little girl. Warren who you have measured all men against your entire life. Warren, the love of your life. It can't be over!" Esther chewed on her thumbnail and stared out the diner window. "Where does he live?"

"I don't know," Anna said. Although she could remember

every detail of her afternoon tea with Warren all those years ago, she hadn't paid attention to how she had gotten there. And even if she had, it had been thirteen years and she had been only eight years-old. What eight year-old pays attention to street signs from the back seat of a car?

"Even if she knew, Esther, what do you expect her to do? Show up uninvited? Then what? Knock on the door and say, 'Oh, hello there. Remember me? I left you on the street all by your lonesome,'" Phoebe chortled.

"If only you had a reason, some sort of excuse to see him again," Esther said, ignoring her sister.

"Well, I do have this." Anna pulled the small package from her reticule. "He dropped it in the theater."

"What is it?" Phoebe asked, leaning forward.

"I have no idea," Anna admitted.

"It's a box from Anderson's," Esther said softly.

"Anderson's Jewelry Store?" Phoebe asked. "How can you be certain?"

Esther raised an arched brow at her sister. "If anyone would recognize the box of an Anderson's engagement ring, it would be me."

Phoebe and Anna exchanged looks. Esther was on her second engagement, and neither Anna nor Phoebe expected it to be her last.

"Engagement ring," Anna stared at the package in her hand. Esther couldn't be correct. She just couldn't.

"Maybe it isn't his," Esther said, squeezing Anna's hand. "The theater is a very crowded place."

The possibility was slight, but still a possibility.

"And who is to say that only engagement rings are packaged in that manner," Phoebe said. "It could be anything. Perhaps a watch for his granny?"

Another possibility. Although, it would have to be a mighty small watch to fit comfortably within the small box.

"What should I do with it?" Anna asked. She rubbed her

thumb along the cotton string tied around the box. The small package no longer held the same romantic intrigue it had moments ago.

Esther shrugged her shoulders and took a sip of her drink. "Open it."

"She can't do that!" Phoebe snorted.

"Why not? Who's to know?" Esther said.

"Phoebe is right. I can't open it," Anna said. "It doesn't belong to me. It–it seems like an invasion of privacy."

"Well, then there's only one thing to do. You'll have to take it to Anderson's Jewelers."

"How will that solve my problem?"

"Well, maybe they will recognize the ring –"

"If it is a ring," Phoebe interrupted.

"If it is a ring," Esther agreed. "But no matter what piece of jewelry the box holds, you have a better chance of returning it to the rightful owner if you take it back to where they purchased it."

"Isn't returning it to the Gladmer a better idea? The person who lost it is more likely to retrace his steps to there, wouldn't you say?" Anna said.

"Do you trust the box office workers at the Gladmer Theater with such a valuable item? No, the owner of that box will assume they have lost it for good and will have to return to the jeweler eventually in order to replace the lost item. When they do, their package will be waiting for them."

"That does seem logical," Anna said.

"Of course it does," Esther said, waving to their waitress. "Now that we've settled that, let's settle our stomachs. I am absolutely famished."

As Anna returned the mysterious box to her handbag, she felt anxious and uncertain. No matter how delicious lunch may be, she felt certain her stomach would feel anything but settled.

～

"I'LL BE right with you, miss," the store clerk said, nodding in Anna's direction. She smiled back and attempted to keep her nerves from showing outwardly as she slowly walked around the little jewelry store. She peered into the glass cases filled with jewels. There were so many to look at, Anna couldn't imagine there being enough customers in the entire world who could afford all those pieces. Many of the items, though fashioned for the more modern crowd, reminded her of some of the jewelry her mother once owned.

"Well, my dear, how might I assist ya today? Are ya looking for yerself, or a gift for a loved one?" The man's well-wrinkled face crinkled at the eyes as he spoke from behind the counter.

Anna returned the man's smile. "Neither." She found herself quickly relaxing in the presence of the elderly gentleman.

His wrinkles at his receding hairline deepened as he looked at her, clearly confused. "Well, if you're sellin' somethin', we aren't interested. The sign on the door clearly says no solicitin'."

"Oh, no," Anna said, shaking her head. "I'm not selling anything. I was hoping you could help me. You see, I've found something and a friend believes it was purchased here. I was hoping you could find the owner and return it?"

"Found somethin', ya say? Might I see it?"

Anna pulled the small box from the Dorothy bag hanging on her wrist. She handed it to the gentleman.

"Well, it certainly is one of my boxes," he said proudly. "No one but Anderson's wraps them in paper like this."

"That is what my friend said. She thought you would be able to help me."

"Well, I can identify the box, but I'm not so sure of the contents. We sell a lot of jewelry, but some pieces are special. Let's take a look, shall we?" He ripped into the paper. Anna started to stop him, but kept to herself. How else would they discover the owner, and the contents did once belong to the jewelry store, so it didn't seem improper for him to look. She watched anxiously as his gnarled hands laid the torn paper aside and turned the box over. The box beneath the paper was made of navy blue leather stamped with a gold inlay border and a matching gold latch. The box itself was a piece of art and Anna wondered why in the world the store would cover that beauty with what she considered a rather plain looking paper and simple cotton string.

He pressed the gold latch and the box snapped open. She yearned to lean over the counter and see what it held, but another part of her dreaded the truth.

"Ah," he said. "Yes, yes indeed. I do in fact remember this piece. A special order, this one."

"A special order? Am I to assume that you don't get many of those?"

"Oh, we get special orders, but not like this one. This order was one I won't soon to forget. Mr. Mallory was very specific about this one."

"Mr. Mallory?" Anna repeated. Her heartbeat pulsed in her throat.

"Yes, he was adamant that there be exactly thirteen small diamonds surroundin' the center stone. Said he didn't care what the cost, there had to be thirteen."

Diamonds. Center stone. Anna's heart beat louder. Her temples began to throb. "It must be a very special piece," she said, trying to portray a calm she did not feel.

"Yes, yes," he said, turning the box toward Anna. "But aren't all engagement rings special to those they belong to?"

Anna felt the blood leave her head. If she hadn't believed his words, the breathtaking diamond ring facing her right now was impossible to deny. The box belonged to Warren. And it contained an engagement ring.

Warren was getting married. Her Warren. Her prince. He hadn't come back for her all those years ago, and he wasn't coming now. He wasn't coming ever. He was in love with someone else. But, if that were true, they why did he pursue her at the Gladmer?

"He and Miss Perry make a fine couple. I hafta admit, I was surprised that after all this time, he was finally proposin', but with the war looming over all these young men's heads, it's no wonder I've been overrun with engagement ring orders."

The elderly jeweler was speaking, but Anna heard none of it until she felt him press the box, repackaged in a new shell of almond covering, into her hand along with a scrap of paper. She looked at the paper. Written on it was an address she didn't recognize.

"I'm certain Mr. Mallory will be relieved to have his missing ring returned to him. You might even receive a reward."

A reward? "Oh, no, I can't. I came here to give it to you."

"Me? But it belongs to Mr. Mallory. It needs to be returned to him."

"Yes, but couldn't you return it?"

"I'm sorry my dear, but as you can see, I am the only one in the shop. I cannot close down just to deliver a package. Don't worry, it isn't a far trip by cab. Here," he said, placing some money in her hand. "This should be more than enough to get you there and back."

"But, couldn't you deliver it after your store closes?"

"My dear, I'm not certain how long you've had the ring in your possession, but can you imagine the stress Mr. Mallory must be under? And I have no idea when he intended to present the ring to Miss Perry, but I would think he would like it returned to him as soon as possible."

Anna stared at the box in her hand. "I suppose you are right," she said. A bell jingled near the door behind her, signaling another customer's arrival.

"I do appreciate your help, but I must get back to business," the little old jeweler said, winking at her. "I do hope the reward is great."

Anna walked by several cabs, still clutching the money in her hand. She walked the few blocks to her home in a fog, not really certain of what she was going to do, but certain that taking a cab to the home of Warren Mallory was most possibly the worst idea she had ever heard.

ANNA TOSSED the box and money onto the table and removed her gloves. She scowled at her reflection as she ripped the pins out of her hat and threw it on the table as well. She sucked the knuckle of her index finger, glad her mother wasn't present to chastise her for the childhood habit, as she paced the room. It took no time at all in the confined space, and she grew almost dizzy at the circles she was walking.

"This is ridiculous," she said out loud. "This will get me nowhere." She plopped herself onto a dining chair, placed her elbows on the table and rested her head in her hands to pray.

"Lord, I don't know what to do. I don't want to take this to his house."

Not your will, but Mine.

"Of course, Lord, but you can't possibly mean that I have to actually deliver it in person."

Let us not become weary in well doing

"I know Lord, but…"

Do that which is good

"I want to do what is right, but there must be some other way."

Him that knoweth to do good and doeth it not, to him it is sin.

Sin. Anna hadn't thought about it that way. But scripture was very clear on the matter. She knew what was right, to return the box. But she couldn't bear to see Warren again, not now that she knew the truth.

She lifted her head and her eyes settled on the doll staring at her. She rose from her seat and took Gertrude off the bookshelf. Her green evening gown was worn and faded from years of love and play, but the beauty of what it symbolized was brighter today than when it was brand new.

Had it really been thirteen years since that fateful tea party with Warren? She had been so young, yet the crispness of the details she remembered made the memories seem so much more recent. She could still feel the heartache she felt when her father had told her they would not return to retrieve her doll. To Anna, Gertrude was her best friend, her confidant, her partner in crime. She wasn't just a doll that could be replaced, as her father suggested. She was family and abandoning her like that felt horrifying.

She had cried for days. Her mother allowed the sadness for the first day, but insisted that Anna brighten herself and accept her father's decision without another tear shed. So, Anna held her tears in front of her parents, but when alone, when she missed Gertrude the most, they fell freely as she mourned the loss of her best friend.

It was the fourth day since losing her doll. Father had left that morning on a business trip, so her mother and she had lunched alone that rainy day. She remembered the rain. Her little girl heart thought it was God's way of saying He understood her pain, that He was crying as well.

They were just finishing lunch when the butler entered the dining room.

"There's a gentleman at the door, madam."

"Please tell him that Mr. Gibson is away on business and should return on the morrow."

"He isn't here to see Mr. Gibson."

"A gentleman is here to see me?"

"No, madam. He is asking to speak with Miss Annabelle."

Anna looked at her mother who stared back at her, one eyebrow raised. She wasn't certain, but she hoped she was right. There was only one gentleman Anna wished to call on her.

"Anna!" her mother called after her, but she had already fled the dining room to race toward the front hall. She reached it in seconds and there he was, brushing off beads of rain that had gathered on his shoulders.

"Warren!"

She saw him smile only seconds before she threw herself at his hip and wrapped her arms around his waist. She heard him laugh as he patted her shoulder.

"Annabelle!" her mother exclaimed. Her eyes flitted frantically between Warren and the bundle of energy that had attached herself to his side.

"Mumma!" she exclaimed, not relinquishing her hold on him. "This is Warren!"

"Oh, I see." Elizabeth Gibson smiled and folded her hands in front of her. "But a lady never throws herself at a gentleman, my dear."

"Oh, of course," she said, finally pulling away from him. She curtsied and said, "It is so nice to see you again, Mister Warren."

"The pleasure is all mine, Princess Grace," he said, bowing.

"Grace?" Elizabeth Gibson looked at Warren with a slight frown. Before he could answer, Annabelle leaned over and whispered to her, "That's what he likes to call me. It's his pet name for me. You know, like father calls you darling?"

That explanation was met with another "Oh, I see," from Elizabeth and a smile from Warren. Once she had cleared that confusion, she turned her attention back to her 'beau.'

"Oh, Warren, I thought I'd never see you again. My father said we were not allowed back in your house," she said, drawing a gasp from her mother. Anna knew that it was probably improper to tell others the things that her parents spoke of within the confines of their home, but this was Warren. "I thought that our courtship was at its end," she added dramatically.

To his credit, Warren did not react to her disclosure or to her mother's gasp. He smiled at Elizabeth as he knelt in front of Anna.

"I do apologize for not calling sooner, dear princess, but I was busy commissioning a present for you," he said, pulling the doll from behind his back.

"Gertrude!" she said, reaching out and touching the tips of the doll's new dress reverently. "It's beautiful."

"I'm so glad you like it." He handed her the doll. "Do you know that not a single shop in all of Lansing carries evening dresses for dolls? I finally found a place willing to make one. That's why it took me so long to return her to you."

Annabelle Grace hugged the doll close to her chest and smiled at Warren. "I've always wanted an green evening gown."

"Well, then someday, when you are old enough, you shall have one," he said.

"Won't you stay for some tea?" her mother asked.

"Oh, yes! Yes, please, Warren! Please stay for tea!"

"I'm sorry, but I can't." He rose to his full height and towered over the tiny princess. "I have to finish packing."

"Packing?" Anna's enlarged eyes blinked rapidly. "Where are you going?"

"That's the other reason I came...to say goodbye. I leave for boarding school tomorrow."

"Will – will I ever see you again?"

"Of course. I will come around every time I am home on break. And I will write. Would you like that? Would you like me to write to you, Princess Grace?"

"Oh yes, Warren. Please write to me," she clapped enthusiastically. Then, as if captured by a thought, she grew serious. "Warren, I hope you understand that I cannot wait for you. Boarding school is so very far away and I am sure there will be other gentlemen that will want to court me."

"Oh, I am certain there will be," he said just as seriously.

"But when you return, if I have not married, then we can renew our courtship," she nodded emphatically, offering her hand to Warren.

"Anna!" her mother gasped, covering her mouth with her hand. Warren smiled.

"I look forward to our next meeting, dear princess." He bent ceremoniously and kissed the offered hand.

Anna leaned in when Warren bent to kiss her hand. "I will wait a lifetime for you, Warren Mallory," she whispered before he lifted his head. Warren winked at her, then turned and walked out of her life.

Anna smiled remembering that afternoon. It was her last happy memory in that house, because that rain that had seemed to sweep Warren and Gertrude back into her life was the same rain that also made the roads between Detroit and Lansing dangerously muddy. The same rain that took her father away from her.

The doll was so much more than an old toy. It was a symbol of love. The love of a father who had brought it home to his only child. The affection of a young man toward a little girl. Warren had had no obligation to return Gertrude to Anna, yet he hadn't thought twice about doing so. What had he sacrificed for her? Had he worried how he would be received, knowing their fathers had argued so heatedly? And the dress. Not only had it cost him money, but it had cost him time as well. As a child, Anna had loved the beauty of the dress. As an adult, she appreciated the beauty of the heart behind the act.

She hugged Gertrude to her chest, like she had done so many times following her father's death. Warren had made that sacrifice all those years ago, having no idea what it would mean to a little girl about to lose her father. For that, she could never thank him enough. She would return the ring, no matter what sacrifice it took on her part. Just this once, the princess would save the day for the prince.

5

MR. MALLORY'S RING

*A*nna smoothed her skirt as she stepped from the cab. She had no idea why she had changed her dress or why she had taken so much care with her pompadour when she was only going to cover it with her hat. She only intended to hand the box to the butler and leave, and had instructed the driver to wait for her with that plan in mind.

As she climbed the steps of the Greek revival mansion and stared at the front door, everything in her screamed for her to run, but God would not allow it. She knew what was good, and she was going to do it. She lifted a shaking hand and knocked on the door. She knocked so lightly that she wondered if she should try again, but within seconds, the great door swung open to reveal a tall, thin man with a square chin and receding hairline, his stiff black suit the only thing more serious than the look he gave Anna ... the butler. And not just any butler, but the same butler that had been in their employ all those years ago! Something in Anna relaxed at the sight of a familiar face.

"Oh, hello," she said, relieved. She smiled at him, forgetting her mission for the moment. The butler's brows lifted as he waited for Anna to speak.

"Oh, yes, of course you don't recognize me," she laughed. Unlike him, she had changed considerably since they last met.

The man's brows snapped together. "Should I?"

"Of course not. How very silly of me. I'm sorry to bother you—"

"Do come in," he swung the large door wide and stepped backwards.

"No, I mean, I only…"

The butler continued his backward motion until he was so far into the home, Anna had no choice but to follow him in order to be heard. Once inside, he shut the door behind her before she had a chance to stop him.

"Now, miss, I assume you are not here to see me, so why don't we begin with your name and with whom you hope to gain an audience."

"Mr. Jameson, would you be so kind as to bring some tea around. I have grown quite thirsty waiting all this time for Mr. Mallory."

Anna turned toward the voice and found herself face to face with the most beautiful woman. She guessed her to be about her age, maybe slightly older. She didn't remember Warren having a sister, but it was definitely a possibility.

"Certainly, Miss Perry," the butler said. He slipped through a door down the hall, leaving the two women alone.

Miss Perry. The jeweler's words returned to Anna. *"He and Miss Perry make a fine couple."*

This woman was not Warren's sister. She was beautiful, with dark brown hair piled atop a head that boasted a perfect complexion and gentle brown eyes. Why wouldn't Warren want to marry a beauty like this.

Anna wasn't certain what to say. She hadn't thought about anything beyond handing the box to the butler and returning home. The woman saw Anna and approached her.

"Hello. I didn't see you there." She extended her hand and smiled. "I'm Patricia."

"I'm Anna," she said, accepting her hand. "Anna Drowne."

Where had that come from? Anna had never been one who lied easily. Deceptively using her mother's maiden name came as a surprise to her.

"Well, Anna, please pardon my bluntness, but why are you here?"

What was she to say? She couldn't tell the truth and risk ruining the proposal. As heartbroken as she was over the thought of Warren marrying another woman, she felt no ill feelings toward her and did not want to spoil the surprise.

"She is here to end my torment," a voice said from behind her.

Anna whirled around to find Warren walking toward her. Where had he come from? Had he been in the drawing room all this time? A slow, easy smile spread across his face as he slid his arms into his coat. His chestnut brown hair was in a disarray as if he had just woken. She had never seen him in an unkept state, but the effect made his boyish good looks even more endearing.

"Torment?" Patricia said. Anna turned back to her, praying God would either give her words suitable for the situation or would strike her dead, death seeming the lesser evil at this moment.

"Yes, torment," Warren whispered, moving to stand between the two women, but facing Anna. "Do you know how difficult it is, Miss Anna Drowne, to locate a person when you know nothing about her, not even her name?"

"You—you tried to locate me?"

The corners of his mouth turned up, giving him such a boylike charm that Anna's knees began to weaken. "Of course I did, but obviously my detective skills aren't as sharp as yours. You have no idea what it means to me that you came looking for me," he said.

Her heart raced. This wasn't a dream. Warren, in the flesh, was in front of her. If she reached out, she could touch him, smooth the hair that had fallen over his forehead, caress his cheek. A movement over Warren's shoulder caught her eye. Miss Perry was still there. Warren's Miss Perry.

"I–I think I have something that belongs to you," she stammered, trying to remember that this man was not a man for her to daydream about.

"Something that belongs to me? I'm sure I have no idea what that could be." He smiled provocatively, stepping even closer to her. "Unless you plan to return the heart you so callously stole from me," he whispered, stopping only inches away.

Anna needed no mirror to tell her that the tingling sensation she was feeling in her cheeks meant that she was blushing, nor did she need anyone to tell her that the pounding in her ears was her own heartbeat racing out of control. She should not feel this way about a man that belonged to another. How could her body betray her like this? More importantly, why was he doing this? Did he not realize that his fiancé, or soon to be fiancé, stood several feet behind him watching his every move with a frown on her face?

"Are–are you seriously flirting with me? In front of her?" she whispered.

He raised a devilish eyebrow. "Did you wish to go someplace more private?"

"Excuse me, Mr. Mallory, but will Miss Anna be joining you and Miss Perry for tea?" the butler asked, entering the room once more.

"No," Anna said.

"Yes," Warren said at the same time. "No?" he said turning back to her. "Surely you haven't gone to all the trouble of finding me only to turn around and disappear into the night again?"

He hadn't whispered this last statement and Anna was mortified to think that Patricia Perry had heard her boyfriend say Anna had sought him out. It was too much for her. Cheeks hot with embarrassment, she shook her head. "I'm sorry. I've made a mistake." She turned and rushed out the door.

Anna flew down the front stairs to the sidewalk. Without waiting for the driver, she reached for the handle of the cab herself and opened the door, but before she could fling herself into the car, Warren was there.

"Stop!" He grabbed her elbow and turned her to face him. "Where are you going?"

"Where am I going?" She tried futilely to wrench herself from his grasp. "The question is, why are you following me? Surely you must see how this looks?"

"How this looks? I wish I knew," he said, laughing. "A woman I barely know shows up to my house for an unknown reason, flirts with me momentarily, then rushes off without another word. Seems to me 'Where are you going?' is a perfectly appropriate question."

"Flirts with *you?*" *The nerve of him!* "I did no such thing!"

"Well, I do suppose I was the one flirting," he said with a shrug. "But in my defense, what else is a man to do when a beautiful woman hunts down his address and shows up unannounced. It is rather unorthodox, wouldn't you say?"

"Yes," she said quietly, mortified by her own actions. "Yes, it is. But, I had to see you again."

At this, Warren finally released his hold on her elbow. But any relief Anna may have experienced was short lived as his hand now cupped her chin, forcing her to look him in the eye.

"You've made me a very happy man with those words," he said, lowering his voice. "It has been torture these last few days, wondering what happened to you, wondering why you didn't meet me, yet having no way to find you."

The huskiness of his voice caused a tremor of warmth to rush through her body. But the feeling his words caused could not make her forget that Warren Mallory was soon to be engaged to Miss Patricia Perry. The man that now held her face in his hand was not the same Warren of her little girl dreams. This Warren was a heartless scoundrel.

Anna glared at him and raised her chin. "And why on earth would you be looking for me?" she hissed through her teeth.

Warren blinked at the change in her demeanor, but then laughed. "Why? I should think it rather obvious."

"Well, it isn't obvious to me. Why would a man in – in your position come looking for me?"

"Well, I assume for the same reason you came looking for me."

"I sought you out to return an item. Nothing else."

"Are we still talking about my stolen heart?" he asked with a wink.

Anna's eyes narrowed. "I have your missing box."

"My missing what?" he asked, a look of confusion replacing his smile.

"Your box. You dropped it at the theater the other night. Surely you have noticed it was missing."

"My dear Miss Drowne, I am sure I have no idea what you are talking about."

Anna reached in and pulled the small, wrapped box from her purse. She held out her hand.

"This is what I'm talking about."

Warren looked at the package blankly. "It isn't mine."

Why was he lying to her? Did he still hope to hide the truth from her?

"I know that it is. I took it to the jeweler and he identified it as the engagement ring you had commissioned from him."

"That I had commissioned?" Warren said incredulously. "I did no such–wait a minute…" Warren rubbed the back of his neck. "You said I dropped this at the theater?"

"Yes. Someone found it in my box and thought I had dropped it. I planned on giving it to you after the performance, but that didn't work out."

"And you opened the box and saw an engagement ring?"

"No! Oh, no! I would never open someone else's property!"

"Then how do you know what's inside?"

"The jeweler opened the box, to see if he recognized the item. Then he wrapped it again."

"I see. And I suppose this jeweler told you that a Mr. Mallory commissioned this particular piece of jewelry?"

"Yes. That's what I just said."

"And, of course you were instantly shocked and angered that the man you had so recently became smitten with was in fact about to promise himself to another woman."

"Smitten!" Anna shrieked a little too loudly. She bit her bottom lip and took a deep breath. "You are a cad. Please take this box so I can be finished with this whole affair."

"Oh, no. You are far from finished with this affair, my dear." He grabbed her other hand and turned back to the house.

"Let go of me!" she screeched as quietly as she could. "What–What are you doing?"

Warren said nothing more, just continued dragging Anna behind him until they were once more inside the large hall. Patricia was still there, looking more confused than when Anna had left. The butler entered carrying a tea tray.

"Jameson, where is George?" Warren asked.

"In the study. But–"

"Thank you," Warren said to the servant without pausing. Mortified, Anna tried to carry herself in as dignified a manner as possible when being treated like a forgotten rag doll, but she realized she had little dignity left at this point. Warren passed two more rooms, a dining room and what looked to be a parlor of some sort before opening a third door without knocking. In one swift motion, he swept Anna into the room and very solidly shut the door behind her. They looked all around, but saw no one else. To add to her mortification, Anna now realized she, a single woman, was alone in a room with Warren.

"George?" Warren called, maintaining his hold on her hand.

Anna gasped when seemingly out of nowhere, the head of another handsome man popped up from behind the desk.

"What on earth are you about?" Warren asked the man.

"Oh, don't bother me now. I'm in a terrible mess," George said. He returned to his hiding spot behind the desk.

"Looking for something?" Warren laughed.

Again, the handsome head popped up, but this time with a hint of anger.

"How did you know?" George asked, rising to his feet. "So help me, Warren, if this is some sort of prank…"

"Now, hold on," Warren interrupted, holding his hand in the air. "I am not the cause of your woe, but I do believe I have the cure for your ailment. May I present Miss Anna Drowne. Miss Drowne, this is my brother George. Mr. *George* Mallory."

George's eyebrows raised in shock seeing Anna standing there.

"Goodness, I'm so sorry. I didn't even see that you…I am sorry," he said, rounding the desk and nodding toward Anna. "It is a pleasure to meet you, Miss Drowne. I do apologize for being so distracted. I've just lost something very important, and I'm at my wits end looking for it."

Realization dawned on Anna as she looked slack-jawed from Warren to George then back to Warren, whose wide grin showed that he was enjoying Anna's predicament far too much.

"You–you are Mr. Mallory."

George chuckled. "Yes, well one of them, I suppose."

"And, this is yours?" she said, extending her hand and exposing the mysterious package. George's smile faded and his eyes grew wide. Within seconds, he had crossed the room and was snatching the box from her.

"Where…how…?"

"Apparently," Warren laughed, "I wore your evening coat to the theater the other night. I told you it was bad form to choose the exact same coat as your brother. This was bound to happen eventually."

"I don't understand," George frowned.

Anna started to explain when the door of the study was thrown open and in walked the beautiful woman.

"Patricia!" George said, hiding the box behind his back.

"Oh, so you do remember my name! I wasn't certain you knew who I was anymore. After leaving me in your brother's company all afternoon, I assumed you had forgotten all about me. But now, dear George, do tell… who is this mystery woman that is here to see you?"

"This woman? Oh, well, you see—"

"She isn't here for George," Warren interrupted. "She is here for me."

If she could have made her way to the window, Anna would have jumped out of it and ran until her shoes fell apart.

"Oh, really? She didn't seem too pleased to see you earlier. She couldn't get away from you fast enough. Then you drag her back and take her straight to my…George, I demand you tell me right now who this woman is."

Anna watched George struggle to not only come up with an explanation, but to keep the package hidden from view. She felt terrible. Never in her entire life had she been the source of such turmoil. How could she have caused such a commotion?

"I assure you, I have only just met Geor – Mr. Mallory this moment. I came looking for this Mr. Mallory," Anna said, lifting the hand that Warren still held.

"And I was the one looking for George. He owes me money," Warren said.

"Owes you money?" Patricia turned to Warren.

"Yes." Warren released Anna's hand to casually stroll behind his brother. She watched as he patted his brother heartily on the shoulder. To anyone else in the room, it was an innocuous gesture, but as she watched Warren's hand quickly drop behind his brother then casually into the pocket of his own jacket, Anna knew exactly what had just occurred. Warren was now in possession of the box. "Yes, he owes me money. Twenty dollars to be exact. Isn't that right, little brother?"

Anna saw George's jaw tighten ever so slightly as he watched his brother out of the corner of his eye.

"Twenty dollars!" Patricia shrieked, her eyes darting back and forth between the two brothers.

"Yes, isn't that so, George?" Warren had returned to stand beside Anna now, but she knew without looking at him that he was smiling. George, however, was not.

"Yes. Yes, that is true," George said slowly, his eyes boring into Warren.

"Yep, and I came to ask for the return of my money."

"Right now?" George asked, eyebrows raised.

"Why, yes. I need it to take Miss Drowne out this evening. So, pay up dear brother," Warren said, turning and winking at Anna.

Warren was clearly enjoying every minute of the situation. Without another word, George pulled out his wallet and withdrew the sum of money. He crossed the room and handed it to his smirking brother.

"Pleasure doing business with you," Warren said, stuffing the bills into his pants pocket.

"The pleasure is all yours," George said behind gritted teeth.

Anna looked beyond the brothers to the still confused Miss Perry. She stood quite still with her hands clasped casually in front of her, but her eyebrows furrowed intensely above her chocolate brown eyes. She said nothing, but Anna was positive there would be a discussion later between Patricia and *her George*.

"Well, now that that is settled, how about that tea?" Warren suggested.

Before Anna could protest, he grabbed her hand and placed it in the crook of his arm and lead her out of the study. Once in the hall and out of earshot of Patricia, Anna turned to Warren. "I'm sorry, but I cannot stay for tea. A car is waiting for me…"

"Mr. Jameson?" Warren called to the butler standing near the front door.

"Already taken care of, sir," he answered.

Anna looked back and forth between the two men as she was led to the first room off the entry and wondered how they communicated so much with so few words. "Taken care of?" she asked.

"Jameson has sent the car away."

"But I – I haven't paid. How – how am I to get home?"

"Miss Drowne, you can trust that you will be safely returned after our date."

Date? He wasn't serious, was he?

As Warren turned and led Anna into the drawing room, she wondered how she had gotten herself into such a mess, but more importantly, she wondered how she was going to get herself out of it.

6

THE DATE

*W*arren led Anna to the middle of the room where a tea set rested on the sofa table separating the settee from two small upholstered barrel chairs. As she sat, she looked at the pink chair sitting in the corner. It seemed much smaller than she had remembered, but, then again, she was much bigger now.

Warren sat on the settee next to Anna and rested his arm on the back. He didn't lean in, but the comfort he felt at being so familiar with her seemed strange. If she were to be honest, though, it was exhilarating. She knew she should protest, insist that Warren sit in a chair opposite her, but how would that look to Patricia? Wouldn't she expect Warren to sit next to his date? However, she didn't want him to think she was a forward kind of woman. The sound of Patricia and George nearing stopped any argument she might have voiced.

"I still don't understand why on Earth you would ever need to borrow that much money from your brother unless you had gotten yourself into some sort of trouble," Anna overheard Patricia say.

Warren dipped his head toward her ear and whispered. "My brother is going to have to think quick on his feet."

"Was it really fair to put him in such a position? Surely you could have come up with a different story."

"I could have," he admitted with a shrug. "But I'm afraid it wouldn't have been half as much fun."

George and Patricia entered and took the seats opposite Anna and Warren.

"Shall I serve?" Mr. Jameson asked. Anna hadn't seen him enter behind the other couple.

Without waiting for an answer, the butler removed the tray from the small table and took it to a sideboard near the entrance. She wished it would have been proper for her to offer to serve, because she could have prepared her tea to her liking. She had never grown accustomed to the taste, much to her mother's disappointment. Elizabeth Gibson seemed to feel as if Anna were somehow rejecting the British part of her heritage whenever she grimaced at the beverage, so Anna had learned to drink the stuff by diluting it with as much milk and sugar as her mother would allow. But today, she would just have to force herself to drink it normally.

The butler began passing out the tea to those in the room without speaking. He gave to Miss Perry first, then the gentlemen, which Anna found odd. Women should always be served first. But, she realized the butler would know how the other three took their tea. He was probably keeping her for last, knowing he would have to ask her. To her surprise, however he didn't ask. When he handed her the cup, she looked at him in surprise, then at her cup. There was so much cream, the tea didn't look like tea at all. The stoic butler gave her a quick nod then left the room.

Anna looked at her hosts who were deep in a discussion of the news from the war front and saw that none of them had witnessed the silent communication between her and the butler. She looked at her cup again, confused. She took a sip and realized that there was not even a hint of tea. Just milk and sugar, exactly how she had drank 'tea' as a child.

"Well, Warren, where are you and Miss Drowne going this evening?" Patricia asked, all signs of distress completely faded.

"Oh, I don't know, probably dinner at Kerns."

"Oh, no!" Anna protested. "I'm not dressed for Kerns."

"Well, couldn't we stop by your place on the way so you could change?"

The thought of Warren 'stopping by' her little room above the bookstore mortified Anna. She had no idea how to answer. Patricia came to her rescue.

"Good grief, Warren, no wonder you are single. You know nothing of women. A woman does not simply "change" for a dinner date."

Warren looked at Anna. "She'll be the most beautiful woman there, no matter what she wears, so what's the difference. Besides, I have twenty dollars burning a hole in my pocket. Kerns seems the best way to spend it quickly," he said, winking at his brother. George's eyes narrowed as he glared silently at Warren, but he said nothing.

Anna started to object when Mr. Jameson entered and interrupted the conversation.

"Miss Florence Perry," the butler announced. He backed out of the way as another brown-haired woman swooshed into the room.

"Sorry I'm late," the woman said, removing her gloves.

"Late?" Warren asked, looking at George. George returned the look wide-eyed with a slight shrug of his shoulders. "Late for what?"

"Well, for dinner, of course, darling. Why else would I—who are you?" Florence Perry blurted out at Anna.

Anna knew she should utilize the manners her English mother had so fervently instilled in her, but something about the woman irritated her. It probably had something to do with the irksome way she referred to Warren as 'darling'. Before she could stop them, the words flowed from her mouth. "I'm Anna, Warren's date for the evening. Who, might I ask, are you?"

Anna knew she should be horrified for having been so rude, but when Warren rested his ankle across his knee and confidently slid his arm along the back of the seat behind Anna, she had to bite her bottom lip to keep it from curling into a smirk as he eyed the woman, lifting an eyebrow. The brunette's eyes flitted from Warren to Patricia, but the remainder of her countenance remained placid.

It was Patricia who broke the silence. "I apologize. When George and I made arrangements for the evening, I suggested Florence join us. I assumed you would have no plans, Warren. I thought we might coax you into coming along."

Warren's thumb lightly traced the skin of her arm where the fabric of her sleeve ended. The hair on her neck stood on end. She tried desperately to concentrate on what Patricia was saying.

"Anna, this is my sister, Florence Perry. Florence, this is Anna Drowne."

The two women nodded to one another.

Florence's eyebrow shot up. "Have we met? You look vaguely familiar to me."

"I don't believe so," Anna answered. "I have *no doubt* that I would remember." Anna smiled innocently as Warren coughed to cover a laugh. *Please forgive me, Lord,* she prayed.

"Well, I'm certain we have," she argued. "And I'm never wrong."

"Your being correct or incorrect is not filling my stomach, and I am starving," George said, rising.

"We can't go out now," Patricia protested. "It isn't fair to Anna."

"Oh, please, don't cancel on my account."

"Anna and I will just stay in for dinner," Warren said casually, drawing gasps from the two brunette women and a deep blush from Anna. He sighed. "Come, now. I'm certain a house full of servants will make for suitable chaperons."

"Servants do not qualify as chaperons, Warren," Patricia scolded. "Honestly, are you trying to scare off Miss Drowne with your boorish behavior?"

"The last thing I want to do is scare you off again," he said only loud enough for Anna to hear.

"No," Patricia continued. "We will all just have to stay in this evening. George, do you think it would be too much of an inconvenience to your staff if we were to announce that we were dining here?"

"Jameson!" George called. The butler walked quietly into the room within seconds. "It seems that we are dining at home this evening, if that wouldn't be too much trouble for Mrs. Gunderson."

"I have already spoken with her. Dinner will be served in half an hour."

Half an hour? Anna wondered how long ago the servant had decided they would dine there.

Anna leaned toward Warren and whispered. "This charade has thrown everyone's evening into a tizzy. I had no intention of bothering anyone, let alone interrupting everyone's plans."

Warren turned his smiling hazel eyes toward her and she realized how closely she had leaned in. She wanted to withdraw, but seemed powerless to obey her own will.

"My dear, you are the best interruption I have ever experienced. Please stop apologizing."

"But everyone else…"

"Will eat dinner, just as they would have done had you not appeared on our doorstep."

Anna looked at George and Patricia who were happily discussing possible parlor games the group could play after dinner and realized that they seemed quite content with the new arrangement. Then she looked at the other Miss Perry. Brown eyes glared back at her. Anna wasn't certain if Florence was angry that Anna had interrupted her plans for dinner or angry that she had interrupted her plans for Warren.

WARREN PULLED the car up to the address Anna had given him. She had assumed he would call her a cab, but when George announced that they were personally driving Patricia and her sister home and that it would be no imposition to drive Anna home as well, she had to think quickly. They arrived at the address and to her relief, all the lights were out. The residents were either out for the evening or already asleep.

After pulling the car to a stop, Warren jumped out and ran around to open her door. He took her hand to assist her, then placed it in the crook of his elbow to lead her to the front door. Anna's heart beat faster with every step closer to the house.

"You needn't walk me any further," she insisted.

"It wouldn't be very gentlemanly if I left you stranded halfway down the pathway, now would it?"

They reached the door and Anna turned to him. The flickering streetlights cast a faded glow across his face, lightly illuminating his smile.

"I had the most lovely evening," he said.

"As did I," she said honestly. "I do hope I did nothing to give away the charade to Patricia. She seems very kind."

"Yes, well we wouldn't want to spoil things for George and Patricia. You understand they are watching us?" His lip twitched mischievously.

Anna glanced quickly to the car and back at Warren. "I suppose, though it's difficult to tell in this light."

"Then you will forgive me for what I must do."

Forgive him? Anna didn't understand at first, but when his arms snaked around her waist and swiftly pulled her close, she knew in an instant what he was apologizing for. Warren's head bent and his mouth claimed hers.

She had never been kissed before, though she had dreamed of it many times, and Anna basked in the realization that her dreams were now reality. She was being kissed. She was being kissed by Warren Mallory.

Gone were the fears of being found by the home owners. Gone were her inhibitions of keeping her true identity hidden. At that moment, all she knew was Warren and the feel of his lips against hers. But just as she felt her body begin to relax against his, the porch light flickered on above their heads and Warren pulled away.

"We've been caught," he said. He no longer seemed the confident jokester. His face held an almost shyness about it that tugged at her heart. He placed his hat on his head and nodded at her. "Good night, Miss Anna Drowne of 173 West Shiawassee Street," he said with a wink before flying down the stairs toward the waiting vehicle.

Anna stood watching as George cranked the engine then jumped in beside his brother. As the car purred, the door behind Anna opened. Before she could react, and a hand reached out and icy fingers dug into her arm. As Warren's car pulled out of sight, Anna was yanked into the dark house. The pulse in her temples nearly burst in fear as she looked into the eyes of the person gripping her by the shoulders. As her eyes adjusted to the dim lighting of the home's interior, she sighed with relief.

"Why did you turn on the porch light?" Anna demanded.

"Do you really think you are the one who should be asking the questions right now?" Esther asked, releasing her grip. "I'm here all alone. I heard movement and whispers on the front porch. Of course I'm going to turn on the lights."

"I'm so sorry," Anna said. "I didn't know what to do when he asked for my address. I couldn't let him see where I actually live. So, I gave him your address."

"Him? Who was—wait one minute! That was Warren? You were kissing Warren on my front porch?"

"Yes! And you interrupted!"

"You are lucky it was me that interrupted! How would you have explained that to my father? Fortunately, everyone is in Illinois visiting Phoebe at college. If I hadn't been sick, I would be there too."

"If you were in Illinois, the lights wouldn't have turned on and Warren might still be kissing me," Anna said dreamily, leaning on the door.

"And then what? Do you think he would have left you standing on the porch, in the dark, without making certain you entered? And if he did, how exactly would you have gotten home at this time of night?"

"I hadn't thought that far ahead. Oh, Esther! Can you drive your father's car? I have to get home before Mother starts to worry."

"Let me get dressed," Esther said, heading up the stairs. "But you had better be ready to share all the details."

7

SACRIFICES

*A*nna fretted the entire trip from Esther's house to her apartment. She knew her mother would have arrived home at least an hour earlier. Missionary Society meetings never went late. Her mother was probably in a frenzy wondering where she had gone, and Anna had no idea what she was going to tell her. After their conversation following the play, she didn't want to upset her mother with talk of socializing with the upper class again.

But to her surprise, Elizabeth Gibson was not pacing. She was reading.

"Did you have fun this evening?" she asked when Anna entered the apartment.

"Yes," Anna answered cautiously.

"What did you and Esther do?"

"How did you know I was with Esther?"

"I saw her drop you off, dear," Elizabeth said, smiling. "A car pulling up at this time of night makes one look out the window."

"I'm sorry if I worried you."

"I wasn't worried. I trust you."

Anna swallowed hard. She hadn't lied to her mother, but omitting the truth about the evening felt worse than actually lying.

"Well, now that you are home, I believe I will call it a night. It has been an exhausting day."

With her heart still racing from the events of the evening, Anna prepared for bed. She tried to do so as quietly as possible so as not to disturb her mother, who had already fallen asleep. She was grateful. Sleeping seemed a struggle for her mother lately. Since their evening at the theater, she seemed on edge and looked more worn out than usual.

On her way to bed, Anna found the source of her mother's angst. Her mother had left her hat setting on the table. When Anna lifted it to put it away, she found the note. At first, she didn't understand. Why was their landlord sending letters to her mother? He had never done that before. Well, not that Anna had been aware of. When she opened the envelope, she discovered that her mother's sleeplessness was not residual anxiety from the theater visit. She was losing sleep over unpaid rent.

How could they have gotten behind? Anna's mother had always been diligent with their bills, and there had been no unforeseen expenses that would have disrupted their budget. Upon closer examination, Anna noticed the amount the landlord was insisting upon. He had raised their rent. Anna dropped into the nearest dining chair. With both of their incomes combined, they barely made enough to cover their existing expenses, but an increased rent bill was not something their income could accommodate.

After she turned out the lights, Anna suddenly felt the weight of the burden her mother had been carrying. No wonder she had been so tired looking. Anna knew she must do something, but she hadn't a clue what, so she did the only thing she knew to do. Anna prayed.

By the time she slid into the bed beside her mother, she

knew what she must do. She just hoped her mother would understand.

∽

"You did what?"

Anna rose and cleared the dinner plates from the table. "I sold my cream linen suit."

"I don't understand," Elizabeth said, following her daughter with the empty tea cups. "You loved that suit. You spent hours on it. Why on Earth would you sell it?"

"To pay the overdue bills."

The teacups clattered together as Elizabeth bobbled them in the sink. Anna began washing the few dishes they had as Elizabeth made her way to the wingback chair and sighed.

"How did you know?" she asked as she slowly lowered herself to sit.

"I found the letter hiding under your hat. Why didn't you tell me?"

"I didn't want to bother you, dear."

"Bother me? I'm not a child, mother. My income helps to pay our bills. You should have discussed this with me."

"I'm sorry. I know. I don't like having secrets between us."

Secrets. Anna was reminded of her evening with Warren. "No," Anna admitted. "Secrets between us are not good."

"If I hadn't kept this secret, you would still have your suit."

"What do you mean?"

"I mean that it was an unnecessary sacrifice. I took care of the rent this afternoon."

"How did you manage that?"

"I sold my brooch."

"Your brooch? But, it was your last piece of jewelry!"

"Events of late have made me realize that the sentiment I held for the piece was so misplaced. It was actually freeing to let it go."

"Oh, Mother, I wish I had known. It pains me to think that you have had to make yet another sacrifice."

"I was happy to do it. It is you that shouldn't have had to make such a sacrifice."

"It wasn't so bad. Honestly, it felt good to see someone admire something I designed. In the shop, all my work feels so methodical. The patterns we use, even the newest, smartest ones, are created by someone else. No matter how beautiful the finished product, it still isn't mine. I'm not certain if you can understand this. Honestly, I'm not certain I fully understand, but this piece, this felt like an extension of myself, and to see someone truly appreciate it was very gratifying."

"Then, I suppose God allowed this misunderstanding," Elizabeth said. "This joy in your work only came about because of it. Sometimes we have to give up what we hold most dear, empty our hands so they are open for God to fill them with something greater. You gave up your suit, and God replaced it with joy."

"And you gave up your last piece of jewelry. What did God replace your brooch with?"

"The Lord works all things together for good to them that love Him. I'm sure something good will come of it."

APRIL HAD BEGUN like a stubborn hinge, rusted tight and unwilling to open its doors to the days of spring that knocked for entrance. But today, spring had won the battle. The sun shone brilliantly over the city of Lansing, awakening creatures of all sizes, including Anna. The beautiful weather was the perfect excuse to escape the dingy hole from which she normally worked. Miss Leonne's latest dress was finished, so it reasoned that she should take a walk down Washington Avenue to deliver it in person.

The delivery took no time at all, and Anna took her time

perusing the windows of the shops that lined the road opposite the Gladmer that led back to Mrs. Trudy's shop. A slight gust of wind attempted to dislodge her hat, and as she reached to right it, she thought she heard someone calling her name. She stopped and turned about. Residents of Lansing flitted about like springtime robins, but none of the crowd seemed to be speaking to her. She heard it again, but since Anna was not an uncommon name, she continued on, convinced she was mistaken.

"Anna," a male voice said breathlessly.

She turned around and found herself once again face to face with Warren Mallory.

"God is smiling on me today," he said, eyes crinkling at the corners.

Her heart beat so loudly that she wasn't certain he would be able to hear her above its pounding. In the previous decade, their paths had not crossed, but in less than a week, she had been graced with his presence three separate times. She tried to take slow breaths and gave him a smile that appeared spontaneously upon seeing him.

"Oh? Are you having a particularly blessed day, Mr. Mallory?" She tried to appear nonchalant and hoped he didn't notice her shaking knees.

"I am now," he said, looking up at the street sign. "We finally meet on the corner of Washington and Ionia."

Anna blushed. Warren had not mentioned the evening after the play until now.

"I'm sorry about that night. I–"

"Walk with me?" he asked.

She knew she should return to work, but she was ahead of schedule for the day and Mrs. Trudy wouldn't expect her to have finished so quickly with Miss Leonne. Besides, even if she had wanted to deny him, she was helpless to resist his endearing charm.

They walked in silence for several minutes. Anna clasped her hands in front of her in an attempt to keep them steady. Warren sauntered along beside her, hands behind his back.

"You've caused quite the stir in the Mallory house, you know," Warren said, smiling down at her.

"Me? What on earth have I done?"

"Your mere presence alone has caused the disturbance," he said. "Apparently, my brother and Patricia have taken quite a liking to you."

"Did they really say that?"

"Among other things. 'She's nice.' 'She's beautiful.' 'Too beautiful for you'…that was George speaking, of course. 'You'd better not foul this one up, Warren,' was the main consensus, though."

Anna laughed. "Do you have a reputation of bungling relationships?"

"I have a reputation of bungling everything. I tend to take life a little less seriously than the other members of my family."

"That's not always bad. I sometimes wish life were a little less serious."

"It's only as serious as you make it."

"Not everyone has the luxury to have that attitude. Tell me, what have you done to gain such a reputation."

"Oh, let me see…I guess I used to be somewhat of a prankster when I was younger. My mother had a way of keeping me in check without choking me, but when she passed, well, I just seemed to find trouble wherever I went. Mostly harmless, little pranks, but enough to drive my father crazy. I once convinced George that mud was our cook's special pudding."

"You didn't!" Anna laughed.

"I did. And much worse, I'm proud to admit. But, when I became a teenager, I fell in with the wrong crowd and the trouble became much less innocent. I'm not so proud of those years."

As they continued walking and Warren shared with her

stories of his youth, Anna couldn't stop thinking about three words he had said — when she passed. Anna hadn't realized that Warren had lost his mother as a child. She longed to tell him about her father, but she couldn't find the words.

"…and when my father finally had enough, he sent me packing to boarding school."

"Ah, yes, I remember — uh," Anna stumbled on her words. "I remember my mother threatening boarding school a time or two."

Warren stopped and turned toward her, one eyebrow raised. Anna's palms grew sweaty. Did he notice her slip of words?

"I can't believe," he began, "you could ever have done anything so bad as to warrant such a threat."

Anna exhaled, releasing a breath she didn't realize she had been holding. "Doesn't every parent threaten boarding school at some point in a child's life?"

"Yes, I suppose so…but I actually deserved it."

She felt herself drift away to all those years ago when the same boy who found himself sentenced to boarding school had first found himself the host of a little girl's tea party. She had difficulty seeing the Warren of her memories engaged in anything short of heroic, let alone unlawful.

"I must hand it to my father, though," he continued. "That was the best decision he ever made."

"Really? I suppose you are going to tell me that it made a man out of you?"

Warren chuckled. "No, but it did make a Christian out of me."

As Anna listened to Warren share about his boarding school experiences, about the professors and students that became so influential in his decision to turn his life over to Christ and the subsequent change it brought to his life, she wondered what kind of man he would be now if his father hadn't disciplined his actions.

"And now?" she asked. "Do you still find trouble easily?"

Warren laughed. "Now? Well, I suppose I would have to look a little harder these days, but it still finds me sometimes. That's the thing about sin. It's always lurking. I guess that's why the Bible says to flee from it. But even though I knew my life had changed, it wasn't so easy convincing my father. Unfortunately, the members of my family have very good memories, so it was difficult to shed that reputation. I tried settling into the life he had planned for me, but that was easier said than done. After a few years of successfully disappointing my father, he and I both agreed it was best if I wasn't an active partner in the family business. I wasn't serious enough for his taste, and I found the day to day workings of the company far too boring. So, when I turned 25 and came of age to inherit the trust left to me by my mother, I invested it in a local newspaper. News is always changing. It never grows stagnant. I find managing something as active and vibrant as a newspaper far more entertaining than anything the automobile industry has to offer."

"Don't let Mr. Olds hear you say that," Anna laughed.

"Oh, he's heard me say it many times," Warren said with a shrug.

A red-winged blackbird darted into a bush they were passing. The barren branches showed signs of leaf buds, but that did little to disguise the nest the bird was earnestly building within the sparse shrub. Anna stopped and peered into the bush.

"Sometimes God's creation just amazes me," she said. When Warren didn't respond, she turned and looked at him. He stood, coat unbuttoned and hands stuffed in his pockets, staring at the ground.

"You aren't angry with me, are you?" he asked. That same boy-like innocence she had witnessed on Esther's porch graced his face now, exposing his vulnerability in a way that made Anna want to caress his cheek and reassure him. It was fascinating to her, the way his self-assured confidence gave way to uncertainty and shyness. Warren Mallory was the most intriguing prince of a man she had ever met.

"Angry? Whatever for?"

"The kiss."

Was he blushing? Anna's heart raced and she had to look away, certain that her cheeks burned even brighter than his. She didn't want to lie, but she couldn't bring herself to admit that she wasn't angry, and that, in fact, she had enjoyed the kiss very much. "I–I…" she stammered.

"Please don't answer that question. If you are angry, I'll apologize, but it will be a lie." Warren lifted his gaze to Anna. "I'm not sorry it happened. And I hope to repeat it in the very near future."

Anna could feel her pulse quicken at his words. She knew she should say something aloof, something to put him off, but she could think of nothing else other than the feel of Warren's lips gently brushing against hers. She hoped he repeated it in the future as well, and she hoped the future were now.

"What a coincidence running into the two of you this afternoon," came a caustic voice from behind Anna. The irritation Anna felt told her who had interrupted the moment before her brain recognized the voice. Would this woman forever be a thorn between Warren and Anna? Anna turned and stretched her best attempt at a smile across her face. Florence Perry returned the smile with an equally forced one. She could be a beautiful woman, Anna mused, if she weren't always opening her mouth and ruining her looks with her words.

"Good day to you, Miss Perry," Anna said cheerfully. "Out for a walk?"

"I'm on my way to the dress shop. That silly girl that works there messed up the dress I ordered. Honestly, you can't find good craftsmanship these days. I should just give up on that place and buy all my dresses at Arbaugh's. I'd save money, I know, and not have to deal with that little twit, but I just can't bring myself to wear a dress that a dozen other women own the match. You understand, don't you darling?"

Darling. How could a name of endearment sound so disturbing every time this woman used it?

Anna knew what little twit Florence spoke of. Irene had unkind nicknames for Miss Perry as well. Anna couldn't believe how long it had taken her to recognize the woman. True, she hadn't had much interaction with her in the dress shop, but the sound of her voice carried throughout the entire shop every time she visited, including the back workroom, and her burning insults were legendary among the dressmakers.

"Not really," Anna answered. "I don't have anything bad to say about seamstresses."

"Then you must tell me the name of your girl, for I fear I may have to drop mine."

"Well, there is a seamstress at Trudy's shop named Irene. I like her work very much."

Florence Perry's eyelashes fluttered rapidly, like a trapped butterfly desperately working to escape the spider's web, but outwardly she gave no other sign of shock. "I'll have to give her a try," she said with another forced smile.

"Good," Warren said. He placed Anna's hand in the crook of his arm. "Now that that is settled, we shall be off. Pleasure seeing you, Miss Perry."

"Miss Perry?" Florence scoffed. "My word, Warren, you act as if we are strangers. Are you trying to lead Miss Drowne to believe that you and I aren't intimates?" she said, lightly swatting at his arm.

"I'm certain Miss Drowne can make her own determinations about the relationships between others."

"Yes." Florence locked eyes with Anna. "Yes, I hope she can."

A chill slid down Anna's spine under the scrutiny of the other woman. But as quickly as the icy glare had appeared, it was gone.

"So, where are the two of you off to?" Florence smiled and batted her eyelashes at Warren.

"We are just enjoying an afternoon stroll," Warren said, covering Anna's hand with his.

"Good. I could use a stroll myself. Dear Anna, you don't mind if I join you, do you?"

The woman was infuriating. Of course Anna minded, but both she and Florence knew she would never say so. What person would be so rude as to do that.

"I mind." Warren tightened his grip on Anna's hand. "Now, if you'll excuse us, Miss Drowne and I will continue our conversation...privately. Good day, Miss Perry."

Anna waited until they had traveled half a block before speaking.

"Warren, you understand how incredibly rude that was, don't you?"

"I've said worse." He looked down at Anna with a particularly amused look on his face. He kept smiling, but said nothing. Anna smiled back, although she had no idea what was making him so happy.

"What do you find so entertaining?" she finally asked.

He kept walking, the shaking of his head the only acknowledgment that he had heard her question. He was adorable, with his Fedora slightly askew and the corners of his eyes crinkled in mirth.

"Come now," she insisted. "Out with it. I've obviously said or done something you find entertaining."

"Endearing, not entertaining," he said, guiding her to a bench that overlooked the Grand River. "You called me Warren."

Anna clenched her eyes shut, mortified at her blunder. For thirteen years, she had thought of him as Warren. Her Warren. Her prince. It was perfectly acceptable in her imaginary world to refer to him by his given name. But in this world, this very real, unimaginary world where Warren wasn't just a little girl's fantasy, she shouldn't be calling him by his first name.

"I am sorry, Mr. Mall-"

"No," he said, holding up his hand. "Please don't do that. Don't go backward. Call me Warren. I like how my name sounds coming from your lips."

"It isn't proper."

"I say it is. Patricia calls George by his given name."

"Yes, but they are courting. We are not."

"We had Monday evening."

Again, Anna's cheeks grew warm. "But that was for Patricia's benefit. We were pretending."

"Were we?" he asked stretching his arm along the back of the bench. "Were you, Anna? Were you pretending to enjoy yourself at dinner that night?" He locked eyes with her, his voice lowering to a mere whisper. "Were you pretending on your front porch?"

He was so near, she could smell the scent of his cologne and felt the warmth of his arm next to her shoulder. His hazel eyes searched hers and she felt herself trapped by his glare. Just when she thought he was going to repeat the events of the porch, he straightened himself and withdrew his arm. Anna wasn't certain if she were relieved or disappointed. She watched as he nervously adjusted his hat, searching for the words to say next. It was adorable how one minute he was a full-grown man, full of confidence and control, and the next, a shy school boy struggling to talk to a girl.

"I wasn't pretending," she said. She heard the words slide effortlessly from her mouth and remembered something her mother had told her once. Lies are difficult to say. The truth always comes easily.

Anna's confession was met with a sigh and a crooked grin from Warren. Honestly, how would she ever keep control of her shaking nerves if he kept looking at her in such adorable ways.

"I'm not very practiced in the art of romance." Warren reached for her hand. "But if you would allow me, I would like to try my very best to woo you."

Anna's heart raced. Surely this was a dream, like all the ones before. Was it truly possible that this Warren was real?

"Since I am as inexperienced as you," she admitted, "I'm sure I will have no criticism of your tactics."

"So, you will allow me to take you to dinner this evening?" Warren asked, adding with a wink, "That is plenty of warning for you to have outfitted yourself in the proper attire, is it not?"

Anna laughed. "It is, sir. Plenty of time. I will allow you to take me to dinner, but you must allow me to meet you at your house."

"But, why – "

"That is my only condition. You must agree, or there will be no dinner date."

"Then, it will be as you say. I will agree to anything you ask as long as you agree to have dinner with me."

The sun that had earlier been the awakening agent for the city of Lansing slid behind a cloud, casting a gray shadow over the Grand River and the park that bordered it.

Warren flicked the rim of his hat out of view and eyed the sky. "Looks like rain. Let's get you home before this hits." He jumped from the bench in time to hail a cab just passing by.

"Oh, but I can't," she said, searching for an excuse. "I–I still have shopping to do."

"Well, come on then," he said holding the car door for her. "Let me at least get you back to Washington Avenue."

Although she knew it would take only a few moments longer to walk, she was thrilled at the idea of sitting in the back seat of a car next to Warren, even if only for a little while. She jumped in beside him, happy that the pending rain had necessitated the cab ride.

Back on Washington Avenue, Anna waved at the departing cab before turning back toward the tiny dress shop. She nearly skipped the ten blocks back to work while swinging her Dorothy bag from her wrist. Anna didn't even notice the rain that had begun to fall in tiny droplets. She didn't think about her mother or about her poverty. She didn't think about all the lies and misconceptions she would have to live in order to maintain this relationship. She didn't think about what would happen if Warren discovered the truth about her circumstances, and she certainly didn't notice that Florence Perry was following her, watching her every move.

8

EXPOSED

"Father, do you remember the day I was expelled from Lansing High School?"

"Oh, I remember that day very well," Winston Mallory said, flipping the page of the ledger. He often brought work home to his study and Warren usually left him alone when he did so, but he felt the need to speak with him in private.

"On that day, you had a meeting with a gentleman."

Winston stopped writing. "Yes. Yes, I do remember that."

Warren pulled the tufted leather chair close to the desk and sat opposite his father. "And that gentleman's little girl waited in the drawing room."

"She did?" Winston said, looking up. "I had no idea. My word, do you think she heard anything?"

"By anything, if you mean what was being said, then no. Only the volume in which it was spoken."

"That's a shame. Really it is. But what of the little girl?"

"She made quite an impression on me, and when she left her little doll behind…"

"Doll, you say? I don't remember anything about that."

"Yes, a little German bisque doll with amber-colored hair, just like the little girl."

"Are you certain it wasn't strawberry blonde? Her mother had strawberry blonde hair."

" No, I remember distinctly. The daughter's hair was darker, more amber…as were her eyes."

"Her mother had amber eyes, so that makes sense."

"Well, when I returned at Christmas, I went around to visit the little sprite, but the house was empty. None of the neighbors knew anything."

His father leaned back in his chair. "That is a mystery I wish I had been able to solve."

"Does their disappearance have anything to do with the argument you and the father had?"

"No, but my search for them does. The father died. Very tragic. I gave the allotted time for mourning to pass, as I knew would be customary for a woman of her breeding."

"Breeding?"

"English."

"That's right," Warren nodded. "I remember her accent now."

"Yes, English. Nobility at that. But when I went to pay my respects, they were gone. I searched high and low for the mother and little girl. I even hired a private detective.

"A real, live Pinkerton, eh?"

"Something like that. He tracked down the paternal grand-father of the little girl. Told my man the pair had moved back to England. So I sent him there."

"What did he find?"

"A dead end. My investigator said she likely returned to her home country to marry. With a new last name, it would be nearly impossible to ever locate them."

Warren tapped his knuckle against his bottom lip as he slouched in the chair. Returned to England. A dead end.

"I can't tell you how that woman has haunted me, day and

night," his father continued. "Even the other night, I swore I saw her, but like an apparition, she disappeared. I know it's just my mind playing tricks on me. It's been thirteen years and I still pray every day that God will help me locate her."

"Why is it so important that you find her?"

"I have something to return to her." Winston crossed his arms. "Why all these questions now?"

"I've met someone," Warren said. "She could almost be the grown up version of that little girl, but that's impossible. This woman is here in Lansing, not England. And if memory serves me right, the little girl's name was Grace."

"It's been so long, I'm sorry to say that I cannot remember the child's name."

"I've always wondered about little Grace. I guess the resemblance between her and the woman has made my curiosity pique again."

"Or maybe your unanswered questions have you looking for signs of the girl where there are none, just like I seem to see visions of the mother everywhere I go."

"You are probably right," Warren laughed. His father returned to his work, but Warren had one more question. "Father, what did the two of you argue about that day?"

Winston tapped the pen against the page he was working on and sighed. "He wanted me to invest in a wheel company he was vested in."

"But you already own a wheel company?"

"That was before. He had a pretty good head on his shoulders and had a good business plan. I knew it was going to be a success if he could just obtain a bit more financial backing."

"Then why didn't you invest?"

"Because I knew I would be dealing with the man on a daily basis, and because of those dealings, I would come in contact with his wife in social settings. I knew it was best if I stayed out of the man's life entirely."

Warren was silent, letting his father's words work their way to the inner recesses of his mind. What exactly was his father saying? He thought he knew, but he didn't want to believe it.

Winston Mallory pushed away from his desk and walked to the window. He spoke with his back to his son.

"I'm not proud to admit that I coveted another man's wife, Warren. Nothing ever happened, mind you, but the minute I realized I was beginning to have feelings for her, I knew that I must retreat. I know she felt it too, because she kept her distance from me as well if ever our paths did cross. The apostle Paul tells us to flee from temptation in Second Timothy, and investing in that man's company would have been the opposite of fleeing. Can you understand that, son?"

Somehow, he did.

"What happened to the company after the man died?"

He turned and looked at Warren. "I bought it."

ANNA WORKED DILIGENTLY beside her mother on a wedding gown. The customer had been very specific about the quality of the embroidery, as well as the abundance. It would take both women working together on the satiny white fabric to finish in time for the wedding. But Anna didn't mind. Things had been progressing nicely with Warren, and working on the gown allowed her to dream about the kind of dress she would one day wear.

"I need to take a walk," her mother announced, rising slowly and rolling her shoulders. "Shall we have lunch in the park?"

"I'm not hungry. I think I will work through lunch today."

Anna hated lying to her mother, but she didn't know how to tell her that she was having lunch with Warren. In fact, she hadn't told her mother anything about Warren. Anna had been able to work her dates around her mother's missionary society teas and prayer meetings she attended. She knew it was wrong, but she dreaded the look of disappointment her mother would give her when she found out. She remembered clearly the look on her mother's face the night of Miss Leonne's opening night performance and she couldn't bear the thought of causing her mother any more pain.

Anna worked for another twenty minutes and was just about to lay the embroidery work aside when Irene popped her head through the curtain that separated the workroom from the rest of the shop.

"Anna?" she asked. "Do you have a minute? I need some help with a customer."

"Of course," Anna said, following her.

"I'm sorry to bother you," Irene said, pulling the curtain aside for Anna to pass through. "But Miss Perry insisted on seeing you."

Anna stopped mid-stride. Wearing her usual, chilling smile, Florence Perry stood in the waiting room of the dress shop. Worse yet, she wasn't alone.

"See, Warren," she crowed. "I told you that you would enjoy my little surprise."

Anna wished that she could move. She willed herself to run, but her body would not obey. She was frozen in Warren's gaze and could not break the spell. What was that look on his face? It wasn't just shock. Was it disappointment? Disgust? She wasn't certain, but she knew it wasn't the boyish grin she had grown accustomed to of late.

"What's going on in here?" Mrs. Trudy asked. *When had she come in the room? Why wouldn't Warren say something.* "Anna? Miss Perry, is there a problem here?"

"Problem?" Florence squawked. "Well, would you consider one of your workers posing as a wealthy member of the upper class to be a problem? What if I told you that same worker was also working behind your back, selling dresses to your customers outside of this shop?"

"No, that isn't true," Anna said, finally finding her voice. She turned toward the shop owner.

"Oh, really?" Florence's squeaky voice continued. "So, are you saying you didn't sell a particular cream afternoon suit to a particular actress that I have on good authority is in fact one of Mrs. Trudy's customers?"

"Anna, is this true?" Mrs. Trudy asked.

"It's not what you think," Anna argued, tears welling in her eyes. A movement near the entrance caught her attention. She turned just in time to see the back of Warren leaving the tiny shop. As he exited, his arm was around Florence Perry's waist.

The throbbing in her ears nearly drowned out the sound of the elderly shop owner, but the words 'fired' and 'pack your belongings' came through loud and clear. In silence, Anna returned to the workroom and gathered what few items belonged to her. She felt Irene's hand rubbing her back, sensed more than heard her tearful apology. But none of it mattered. Not her job or her reputation. All Anna could see in her mind was the look on Warren's face and the sound of his silence.

9

FIRED

$\mathcal{I}$n a dreamlike state, Anna closed her apartment door and fell back against it. She wasn't exactly certain when the tears had stopped. Maybe while she walked aimlessly around the park her mother was supposed to be lunching in. Maybe before then. She didn't know. But, in this moment of silence in the empty apartment, the lack of tears did nothing to soothe the ache in her chest.

She had lost her job, but she didn't care. They would probably lose the apartment as well, but looking around the shabby interior now, Anna had difficulty caring about that. Her mother would likely be furious, but Anna was not concerned about that either. Somewhere in the recesses of her mind, Anna knew she should be saddened at these things, but she wasn't. She felt nothing about them. In this moment, she felt one emotion, and that emotion was pain. Pain like she had never experienced. Not even when her father died had she felt a hurt like she was feeling now. Losing her job meant nothing to her. The humiliation Florence Perry had brought down on her meant nothing. All that mattered was that Warren knew the truth. Warren knew her secret, and he had left her because of it.

All the years she spent dreaming about her prince burned a hole in her heart as she tore her hat from her head, ignoring the pins that ripped from her scalp. Numbly, she left the support of the paint-chipped door and threw herself across the bed. Before today, she wouldn't have admitted that she had actually dreamed of the day that she and Warren could be together, not even to herself. Watching him walk away, his hand resting on the small of that horrible woman's back, was a splash of cold water in the face of her fantasy. What had she been thinking all those years? To pin her hopes and dreams on a man she barely knew, and why? Because he had done something gallant for a little girl? Did she really think that he did it for any reason actually connected to her? No, somewhere deep inside she always knew that he had acted that way out of his own accord, not because he felt anything for Anna.

But now, with the events of the day shining a light of truth on the misplaced childhood crush, it was time to close the cover of the fairytale book in her heart. Warren wasn't the prince she had made him out to be in her child's mind. He was just like every other person from their past – spoiled, rich and unconcerned for anyone that did not fit into their world.

Anna sat up on the bed and took a deep breath. A pile of letters lying on the table caught her eye. She reached for the pile and discovered they were more bills.

Anna paced the tiny apartment, uncertain of what to do next. With every pass, the pile of bills on the table mocked her more and more. What would her mother say when she found that she had been fired?

Anna threw herself across the bed again and buried her face in a pillow. She did the only thing she knew to do in the moment. She began to pray.

My God, I've been such a fool for so many years. Please help me to forget about Warren so I can focus on what is important right now.

She lifted her head and rolled onto her back. She wasn't certain what she was going to do, but she was certain it wasn't going to happen laying here mourning the loss of a job that paid too little to live on. Anna sat up in bed and found herself looking straight at the wardrobe. Her dresses. They weren't much, but maybe they could buy her a little time until she found further employment. She only hoped Miss Leonne found herself in the market for a few used, but very well made, dresses.

"And you just left her...standing there...without saying a word?" Mr. Jameson said, one eyebrow lifted.

"I didn't want to add to her embarrassment. It was Florence's intent to humiliate her, and I didn't want to give her the satisfaction."

"And leaving her to defend herself alone while the man who claims to care for her flees the scene is not humiliating?"

Warren stopped his pacing and stared open-jawed at the butler. He sunk into the nearest chair and dropped his head into his hands. "What have I done?"

"Made quite a blunder, I suppose," the butler answered.

A wave of nausea bubbled inside of him as he looked at Mr. Jameson. "And there's nothing I can do to fix it. I don't know where to find her."

"Didn't you drive her home the other evening?"

"I drove her, but apparently not to her home. I tried returning there today, only to be greeted by a very confused older gentleman. I didn't believe him at first. I mean, why would she lie to me, but when he introduced himself as a pastor and assured me there were no Anna's living anywhere in the neighborhood, what should I assume?"

"I suppose you should assume she doesn't want to be found."

"That's too bad, for I intend to find her," Warren said, jumping up and opening a drawer of his father's desk. "I'll just rehire that private investigator."

"He wasn't very successful the last time."

"I didn't have her name last time," Warren said, continuing to rifle through the papers.

"The proper name would make your task much easier," Mr. Jameson said. He watched Warren silently for a few moments, then shook his head and sighed. "Where did you say you found Miss Anna this afternoon?"

"A dress shop, somewhere on Washington Avenue." Warren shot up. "Why didn't I think of that? The dress shop! Surely the owner knows how I can find Anna!"

"My thoughts exactly," the butler responded calmly. "I have errands to run on Washington. You contact your detective while I question the woman at the shop. Hopefully, one of us will return with an address, or maybe the young woman herself."

"SHE FIRED YOU? Because of the cream suit?"

"Yes. She saw it as stealing her customer."

"But I tried to order one like it through her. She was unable to procure the right kind of fabric."

"I don't know about that…"

"Besides, what should it matter to her what you do in your free time? The suit wasn't created in her shop on her time? It wasn't made from fabric she purchased."

"None of that matters to her."

"It will when she loses my business!"

"There's no need to do that, Miss Leonne. It's still one of the nicest shops in town. There are plenty of good seamstresses that work there."

"I don't want good, I want the best, and for goodness sakes, will you please call me Charlotte!"

The two women heard a knock before the door of the dressing room was thrown open.

"You are never going to believe where I went for— oh, I'm so sorry. I didn't realize you had a guest," said a buxom blonde barging into the dressing room. Anna recognized her as one of the other actresses from the play she had attended.

"Ruby Walters, this is Anna Gibson, my designer."

"Anna!" The woman seized her hand. "What a pleasure to meet you! I was wondering if I would ever receive an introduction. Charlotte appeared to want to keep you all to herself."

"Well, I've decided to no longer be selfish."

"Good. So, Anna, how much would you charge me for a suit just like Charlotte's?"

"Now wait one minute! I didn't say you could have my style, only my designer. But I'm certain that Anna can conjure up something simply perfect for you."

Anna blushed under Charlotte's praise. "Were you interested in an afternoon suit?" Anna asked, turning toward Ruby.

"Not just one, dear. I can't be seen wearing the same suit every day," Ruby answered.

"How many did you have in mind?" Anna asked, a little leery.

"Well, how many days are there in a week," the woman huffed. "Oh, and I am in desperate need of some evening gowns. I'm afraid it has been far too long since I have replaced any of my dresses."

Anna grew nervous. Her mother's wardrobe was plenty of supply to outfit herself and her mother, but would never accommodate a full wardrobe for another person.

"Well, I suppose I could have a suit ready for you by the end of the week, then we can discuss further pieces."

"How long to finish all the pieces I need for a week's trip? I am scheduled for an audition in Chicago in two weeks."

Anna was speechless. She hadn't even a penny to purchase supplies. If she could get Miss Walters to agree to one suit, she could use the money from that sale to purchase fabric for a few more pieces. She would need time to slowly build up her inventory. She struggled for the right words to express this to the actress.

"Two weeks!" Charlotte Leonne said, interrupting Anna's thoughts. Ruby, do you realize how much that will cost you in rush charges? Maybe you should wait until you return?"

"I don't mind paying the rush charge. Besides, I want to look my best for Chicago," she said, turning to Anna. "How much?"

"How much are you willing to pay?" Charlotte answered in her place. "Anna is in very high demand. You'll have to pay dearly for her services."

Anna watched as the other actress reached into her handbag and pulled out a large roll of bills. She quickly counted out several notes and handed them to Anna.

"I hope this is enough to retain your design services. I must run now. Let's meet again tomorrow. You can take measurements and we'll discuss my needs then," she said before sweeping out of the room.

Anna gawked at the wad of bills in her hand. "Do all actresses have this much money?"

"Not all," Charlotte said, returning to her seat at the dressing table. "Only the ones with special gentlemen friends."

Anna's gasp elicited a laugh from Charlotte.

"Don't be so shocked, Anna. It happens all over the world. And women like Ruby Walters are going to spend their money on frivolous things like fashion, so you might as well benefit from it."

"But, what do I do with all of it? I might be a gifted seamstress, but I have no idea how to run the business side of a dress shop. I haven't even any idea where to purchase the fabric. I highly doubt that the fabric counter at the department store will have anything suitable."

"Come with me," Charlotte said, leading Anna out of her dressing room and down the hall. She opened the door to a much larger room filled with rows and rows of gowns and costumes.

"Eugenia?" she called out.

From the maze of fashion, a tiny wisp of a woman appeared carrying several dresses piled atop one another.

"Anna, this is Eugenia. Eugenia, this is a new designer in town. She will need to purchase fabrics. Could you help her?"

The short woman offered a hand from beneath the pile of gowns. "Pleased ta meet ya," she said, shaking Anna's hand vigorously, nearly dropping two of the dresses. "I got all kinds of leftover fabric ya can have for cheap, an' if ya need more, I'm heading to Detroit on Thursday. Yur more'n welcome to join me, if ya like. Lemme hang these back up and I'll show ya my stash an' ya can see if ya like anything I got."

Charlotte grabbed Anna by the shoulders as Eugenia disappeared once again among the throngs of theater costumes.

"Stop looking so shocked," she teased. "Smile, Anna. This is the beginning of your future!"

10

THE LADY AND THE BUTLER

It had been a very long, difficult day for Elizabeth Gibson. Her return from lunch was greeted with the news that Anna had been fired for working with Mrs. Trudy's customers behind her back. Elizabeth immediately knew to whom Anna had sold her cream suit. She wasn't sure if she should be proud of her daughter's ingenuity or angry at her shortsightedness, for now it meant that not only would Elizabeth need to work overtime in order to finish the wedding dress on schedule, it meant that the two women were now to live on just one income. But even with all that had gone on today, it paled in comparison to the shock she experienced when she saw, standing outside her apartment entrance, a face from her past.

"Did Mr. Mallory send you?" she asked her former servant.

"None of the Mallory household knows your whereabouts, nor do they know my location at the moment."

"Oh," Elizabeth said. She looked up at the window above her head. It was closed, indicating that Anna was not home. "Would you like to come in, Mr. Jameson?"

"After you, Madame," he said, sweeping his arm toward the door.

She led the butler up the narrow staircase and through the paint-chipped door that led to the tiny apartment.

"Would you like anything? Some tea, perhaps?"

The butler smiled slightly, but said nothing.

"Of course not," she said, folding her hands in front of her. "But you really shouldn't find it so odd. We are equals now, you know."

"Not in my eyes, madam."

The silence that followed that statement hung over the room like a heavy fog, and Elizabeth became painfully aware of the shabbiness of her surroundings under the scrutiny of her former servant.

"You have me at a disadvantage, Mr. Jameson. When I first saw you, I assumed Mr. Mallory was looking for me. But if he is not—"

"I didn't say he wasn't looking for you. I only said that he didn't send me."

"So, Mr. Mallory *is* looking for me?"

"That is a difficult question to answer. Although I do not believe he currently has anyone in his employ who is actively searching for you, I do believe discovering you would bring him some sort of relief."

Elizabeth Gibson turned her back on the butler. She placed her gloves on the table and began removing the pins from her hat.

"How did you find me?" she asked.

Jameson's raised eyebrows indicated he was surprised by her question, but the expression was gone as soon as it had appeared. "As luck would have it, I saw Miss Annabelle."

"Anna? Where on Earth—"

"She works in the dress shop with you, does she not?"

Elizabeth laughed. "You haven't changed, Mr. Jameson. How is it you know everything?"

"Not everything. I do not know why you have kept yourself

hidden away all these years? Why are you living the life of a pauper, my lady?"

"Well, when your husband dies, leaving you destitute and there is no one to turn to, you learn to survive, even if survival is as a pauper."

"Mr. Mallory searched for you."

"Searched for me?" Elizabeth scoffed. "When? Because I waited. I waited for months, and no one came. Had he come immediately, there would have been no need to search. But he did not. The one who could have changed my circumstances, changed my fortune, he did not come. Why is that, Jameson?"

"I do not know, madam."

"I do." She stared out the window. "He did not come because he did not want to change my fortune, for doing so would change his."

"And, what if he came now?"

Elizabeth spun to face the butler. "Is that what this is all about? Reporting back to Mallory? Are you going to rush back to that mansion of his and tell him all about this hovel, about my calloused hands and wrinkled clothes? Is that your plan, Mr. Jameson?"

"I have no plan, other than seeing for myself that you and Miss Anna are alright."

"We are perfectly fine. I work hard, but that is nothing to be ashamed of. In fact, I am proud to say that I have spent every day of my life giving Anna what she truly needs. She has never gone without food or shelter or love. I have kept God as the center of her world, even when others told me I was foolish. I clung to Him, and I taught Anna to do the same. Everything else in life will fade away, but what we have is eternal. I have my daughter, I have my dignity, and I have my God. Nothing Winston Mallory has to offer could ever compare to the riches I now own."

The stoic butler nodded. "So, you wish to remain hidden."

"I wish to be left alone. I need nothing from snakes I once thought friends. Can you understand that?"

"If he asks me, I will tell him where you are. I will not lie."

"And if he doesn't ask?"

"I cannot answer that which is not asked."

"Thank you, Jameson."

"Are you certain this is what you want?"

"Most certain."

"Very well, then, I will take my leave. My lady," he said, nodding his head.

"Mr. Jameson, I'm no longer a lady," Elizabeth corrected him.

Jameson turned back to Elizabeth. "You are more a lady today than ever before." He bowed to her then disappeared through the door.

WARREN PACED HIS BEDROOM IMPATIENTLY. He had wasted little time contacting the investigator he had employed previously. The man seemed certain that with her name, he would have much better luck finding the girl, but Warren hoped it would be unnecessary. He was banking on Jameson returning with her this afternoon.

But as the day faded and dusk began to settle over the Lansing landscape outside his second story window, he began to have doubts. The owner of that dress shop would know how to find Anna, wouldn't she? He knew the addresses of all his employees at the paper, or at least he thought he did. Paperwork was part of the hiring process that Warren had always left to his secretary. But, the shop was much smaller than the newspaper. Surely the woman would know her address.

It was nearly time for dinner, yet Warren remained in his room. He didn't wish to see anyone this evening, unless it was Anna. Besides, George was likely downstairs with Patricia, and although she could not be blamed for her sister's actions, looking at Florence Perry's sister and being pleasant at the moment was the last thing on Warren's to do list.

Florence Perry. Just the thought of her name caused the bile to rise and burn in the back of Warren's throat. He remembered very clearly the look of triumph on her face as she humiliated Anna. He also remembered very clearly the angry force by which he shoved her out of the dress shop and into his waiting car.

"I'm sorry to give you such a shock, darling, but I knew you wouldn't believe me unless you saw for yourself."

Warren didn't answer her. He cranked the car and jumped into the driver's seat. He was too angry to respond, but Florence was oblivious to both his anger and his desire for silence.

"Besides, that little hussy needed to be confronted with her lies. How dare she treat you like that."

Warren gripped the steering wheel until his knuckles turned white.

"Clearly, she thought she had found her ticket out of the slums. But you can put that all behind you now. I know you'll be able to forgive her someday, being the good Christian that you are."

The thoughts running through his mind at the moment were anything but Christ-like.

"At least you found out before you made any public declarations or such. Can you imagine the embarrassment? Why, we would…why–why are we here?"

Warren pulled the car to a stop and jumped out. He circled to the passenger side and jerked the door open.

Florence struggled out of the car with no assistance from Warren. "Warren, why did you bring me home?"

"Because this is where you belong. Not in my car. Not in my home. Not in my life. Goodbye, Miss Perry," he said before jumping back into the car and speeding away from the contemptuous woman for the last time.

Warren rubbed his temples, willing the headache bubbling below the surface to go away. What was taking Jameson so long?

Warren was just about to call for another servant when someone knocked. To his relief, Mr. Jameson stood on the other side of the door.

"Did you speak with the dress shop owner?" Warren asked anxiously, motioning for the man to enter.

"Indeed, I did."

"And did you get an address?"

"After much coaxing—"

"You mean money."

"Is there a difference?" the butler asked. "After money exchanged hands, the shop owner gave me the young woman's address. But when I went there, I did not find an Anna Drowne, or anyone by the name of Drowne for that matter. The woman at the address was named Elizabeth."

"Elizabeth? And you're sure you got the address correct?"

"Quite certain. It appears the young woman does not want to be found."

Does not want to be found. The words echoed in Warren's ears.

"I don't care," He ran his fingers through his chestnut brown hair. "I want her to be found."

Mr. Jameson did not answer him. He stood silent, waiting for further instruction. When Warren gave none, he sighed. "Shall I assume you will not be dining downstairs, sir?" The butler's eyes scanned Warren from head to toe, taking in his disheveled appearance.

Warren looked down at his clothes. "I'm not in the mood to dress for dinner. Could you have something sent upstairs, please?"

"As you wish," Mr. Jameson said and exited the room.

Warren stared at the closed door, wondering how he was going to keep from wearing a hole in the floor. It seemed incomprehensible that before that evening at the Gladmer Theater, he lived a somewhat happy life, void of much stress or romantic entanglement, and now, after only a few short weeks, his life had been turned upside down by a woman he barely knew. How was this possible?

But it was possible. And he couldn't give up without making every effort to locate the mysterious beauty. Anna was out there somewhere and he wasn't going to stop looking until he found her.

11

A VISIT FROM IRENE

*a*nna was so focused on the hidden ladder stitch she was working on that she nearly fell off her chair when someone knocked on the door. They never had visitors. Anna laid her work aside and went to the door. She was shocked to see Irene on the other side.

"Can I come in?" the other seamstress asked.

"Certainly," Anna answered, opening the door wide.

Irene appeared nervous as she stepped into the tiny apartment. She looked around at all the shabby interior, looking for somewhere to sit.

"I'm so sorry," Anna said. "I wasn't expecting company. Here, let me move some fabric."

"Ya don't need ta fuss fer me," Irene said, twisting the ties of her bag that hung off her wrist. "I only need a minute of yer time."

"You can certainly have more than a minute, Irene," Anna said, smiling at the fidgety woman.

"Please, don't be so nice ta me." She shook her head. "It's all my fault ya got fired. That's why I'm here, ta say I'm sorry. But I promise ya, Anna, I had no idea that Miss Perry was gonna do that. She just kept insistin' that I get ya, said she had something to say to ya." Irene lifted her eyes to Anna's. "I just assumed she wanted to have you as her seamstress and wanted to say it in front of me, ya know? She's mean like that. But if I had known she was gonna do that to ya, I never would have told her you were in the back. I'm so sorry. Really I am."

"Calm down, Irene. It isn't your fault. Miss Perry was out to get me. She would have found a way to hurt me with or without you. Besides, how could you know she had plans to humiliate me like that?"

"You mean it? You ain't mad at me? I was for sure that ya'd be mad at me. I wanted to come sooner, but I was afraid ya didn't want to see me."

"Well, you can put that fear to rest, because I'm not angry. Not with you, not with Mrs. Trudy, and honestly, not even with Miss Perry."

"Ya ain't mad at Miss Perry? Why in the world not?"

"Because, being angry with her will only harm my own heart, not hers. And besides, she just helped me see what I was too blind to see on my own."

"That ya was better off without Mrs. Trudy?"

Anna looked around her cluttered room. "Well, yes, I suppose there is that, but there is more. I thought I could fit into a world that I no longer belong to, a world that deserted my mother and me long ago. But if I learned nothing else that day, I learned that I am not of the same class as Miss Perry."

"Darn right, ya ain't. She ain't got no class at all. You'd outclass her any day of the week, I say."

Both women laughed. "And so would you, Irene. Anyone willing to humble themselves and apologize to a friend, no matter the consequence, is a class act in my book. Are you certain you wouldn't like to sit for a while? Have some tea, maybe?"

"No, I only snuck outta the shop ta—oh, goodness! I almost forgot!" she said, handing a slip of paper to Anna. "Miss

Leonne came by the shop a few minutes ago. She knocked on the back door askin' if any of us knew how to find ya. We all said no, afraid Mrs. Trudy would hear us, but I snuck out after her. She gave me this and asked me to give it to ya."

Anna unfolded the piece of paper.

ANNA,

It is urgent I see you in my dressing room immediately. There's a problem with my latest dress.

~C. Leonne

"A PROBLEM WITH HER DRESS? I wonder what could have happened?"

"I don't know, but she seemed kinda anxious."

"I see," Anna said, pinning her hat into place. "Well, I suppose if doctors can make house calls, so can I."

ANNA KNOCKED on the door and heard a voice from within bid her enter. She slowly opened the door, not knowing what she would find, but to her surprise, nothing seemed amiss. Charlotte Leonne met Anna in the middle of the room wearing what appeared to be a perfectly fine dress.

"My word, Charlotte. By the tone of your note, I expected to see you in tears and your gown in shreds." Anna laughed. "Your dress looks fine, but your countenance is sheer agony. What in the world has you so jittery?"

Charlotte grabbed Anna by the shoulders, then wrapped her arms around her in an embrace. Anna laughed again.

"I'm glad you are happy to see me, but I am still confused as to why I am here."

"Please forgive me," Charlotte whispered before pulling away from Anna and walking toward the door.

"Forgive you? I don't understand," Anna said, turning to watch the woman leave the room. But as the door closed behind her, Anna understood. Behind the door, leaning with his arms crossed, was Warren.

12

AMBUSHED AT THE GLADMER

*R*elief. The only word to describe the emotion that flooded Warren's body right now. He had found her. It had taken nearly two weeks, but he had finally found her. And he had never felt more relief in his entire life.

They stood for several moments staring at one another. Anna's cheeks were flushed and her hair fell in wisps all around her face beneath a hat that had been hastily pinned into place. Warren had never seen a more beautiful woman than the one that stood before him now. He finally broke the silence.

"A seamstress. That explains how you always had the most beautiful clothing – Patricia's words, not my own. I wouldn't know couture from rags."

"Yes," she said, her chin lifting a little higher. "I am a seamstress."

"Why didn't you tell me?"

Anna laughed. "I think your reaction at the shop is answer to that question."

"My reaction was shock, Anna. Nothing more. I was completely astounded that you had lied to me."

"When did I lie about my occupation?"

"You never told me."

"What? That I am a poor seamstress? That I work hard for the money in my pocket? That I'm not a debutante living a life of privilege? No, Warren, I did not tell you."

"If you had told me, you wouldn't have experienced that embarrassment."

Anna snorted. "You mean *you* wouldn't have been embarrassed. Getting fired was the best thing that has ever happened to me."

"Is that what you think? That I was embarrassed?"

"What else should I think? You couldn't get out of the dress shop fast enough."

"I was trying to get Florence out of there."

"Oh, yes. Florence. I bet the two of you had a good ol' laugh at poor, little Anna," Anna said, narrowing her eyes and planting her hands on her hips. "How is dear, sweet Flossie?"

"I wouldn't know. I haven't seen her."

Anna looked at him, shock clearly evident in her eyes. "You haven't?"

"No. I have banned her from the house. Florence Perry's presence in our home was only tolerated because she was Patricia's sister, but no longer. All of the staff has been instructed that she is not to enter, much to their relief."

He watched as her shoulders relaxed slightly. He was beginning to get through to her. Warren took a step toward her.

"Tell me," he said, his voice husky. "Why do you keep running from me?"

The closer he got to her, the more uneasy she appeared. She looked away from him and, as if just realizing how she appeared, reached up and tried to smooth away the stray hairs.

Warren reached for her hand. "Don't. I like it just the way it is."

"I've been busy all day. I must look–"

"Radiant," Warren interrupted, running the back of his

knuckles along her cheekbone. "You still haven't answered me. Why do you keep running?"

"I'm not running. I'm just returning to where I belong."

"Where you belong? What would you say if I told you that I believe you belong with me."

"I would say that you are mistaken," she said, pulling away from his touch slightly. "No, Warren. I don't belong in your world. Your world is full of money and wealth and Florences. Not simple seamstresses like me."

"What do you know about my world?"

"More than you realize."

"If that were true, then you would know that my world is generally filled with meetings and deadlines not dinners and debutantes. On any given day, my hands are more likely smudged with printing ink than adorned with dress gloves. I work as many hours as you do, if not more, for the money in my pocket. If you really knew about my world, Anna, you would know that I am not so different from you."

"But, you are a Mallory. Would you have me believe that your family is not as wealthy as they appear?"

"No, I'm not saying that. My family is wealthy, and yes, I am wealthy, but I don't live the life of a spoiled aristocrat. I decided long ago that I wanted a different life, that God had a different life for me."

"What—what do you mean?"

"Come," he said, extending his hand. "Let me show you."

THE LANSING STATE JOURNAL was unlike anything Anna had ever seen. It was a bustle of activity from the moment they walked in the door, people walking in and out of small offices and various other rooms that Anna couldn't identify. In the background, a low, rumbling hum of some sort of machine echoed through the back of the building. A voice shouted over

the dull roar, but it was too far away to understand. A recep-
tionist jumped from her seat when she saw Anna and Warren, a
stack of small notes in her hand.

"This place has erupted," the secretary said, handing the
papers to Warren. "Baker lifted the censorship on the death
roster."

Warren's brows furrowed. "Where's Nichols?"

"In the back room. The press car is acting up."

Warren quickly thumbed through the messages as Anna
stood watching him. Anna felt more than saw the secretary
watching her. She snuck a glance out of the corner of her eye
and found the woman looking between Warren and herself. The
poor girl was probably wondering who in the world Anna was
and why she was here with her boss.

Anna cleared her throat. Warren didn't notice. She tried
again, but to no avail. She finally gave up and spoke to the
woman herself.

"I'm Anna," she said, extending her hand to the other
woman.

Warren looked up from the notes. "I'm sorry. Miss Drowne,
this is my secretary, Miss Hagerman."

"Pleased to meet you," the woman said, shaking Anna's
hand. She stood expectantly, waiting for more information, but
when Warren returned to reading his messages and gave no
more details on the identity of the woman by his side, Miss
Hagerman left the two and returned to her desk.

"Warren," Anna whispered. "Don't you think she was
looking for a little more information than my name?"

"I'm certain she was, my dear," Warren said without looking
up. "But I wasn't certain what information to give. When you
decide that you can in fact be a part of my world, then I will
know how to introduce you to my coworkers."

Anna's cheeks grew warm. She wasn't certain if it was due
to the bluntness of Warren's comment or his casual use of the
term of endearment that made her blush.

While she pondered this, Warren returned the notes to his secretary and gave her instructions on whose phone calls to return, whose notes to ignore, and with whom she should schedule meetings with him for the next day. The woman nodded, smiled and began carrying out his instructions.

"This way," Warren said, guiding Anna to a large office just off the reception area. He closed the door and showed her a chair opposite the large, boxish desk. He sat across from her, brows still furrowed, staring at the last slip of paper.

"Is everything alright?" she asked.

Warren looked up, startled. "I'm sorry, Anna. I was a thousand miles away just then."

"Where exactly would that be?"

"France," he sighed, throwing the paper on his desk and leaning back in his chair. "The war department lifted the censor order on news from the front. General Pershing is reporting casualties. A lot of casualties."

"How many?"

"750 Americans, according to this report."

Anna sat in silence. She had friends serving in France, schoolmates and church friends. Were any of her friends among those listed? She lifted her gaze to find Warren rubbing his forehead.

"You know, I struggled with the decision to enlist or not. I'm thirty-one. The draft does't extend to me. But as an American, I felt it my duty. But God told me no. He told me my responsibilities lay here, reporting this kind of news to the families at home."

"And this news, the report of all those casualties, does it make you feel like you made the wrong decision?"

Warren took a deep breath. "Every day that I wake in my own bed, eat at my own table, I question if I made the right decision or not. But I'm not frustrated over my lack of participation. I'm worried about George."

"George?"

"He's been drafted."

Anna gasped. "But Patricia?"

"She doesn't know yet. That's why he bought the ring. He wants to marry her before he leaves, so that if he doesn't return, well, she will be taken care of."

They were interrupted by a knock. A young man stuck his head through the cracked door. "Nichols needs ya, Mr. Mallory. Says you'll know what to do with the press car."

"I'll be right there." Warren stood. "Anna, I'm so very sorry, but I am going to have to call you a cab. It seems I have responsibilities here which I must attend to. You understand, don't you?"

"Of course," she said, rising as well. "You're very good at what you do, aren't you?"

Warren shrugged, smiling his boylike grin. "When you like what you do, it doesn't seem laborious. Honestly, the work was much easier when I worked for my father, but I hated it. Addition was about the most strenuous activity that was expected of me. When you own as many businesses as my father does, you have to hire men to manage the various companies. Your job becomes little more than bookkeeper. I got bored, and I'm not a good person when I'm bored."

"Do you become grumpy?" Anna had a difficult time imagining him grumpy.

"No," Warren laughed. "I become mischievous. And I found myself butting heads with my father a lot. He wasn't happy when I bought the Journal, but I think he respects my decision now. I could never spend my life working like my father. But here, it's different. News changes daily, hourly in fact. No two workdays are ever the same. It's harder work, but much more rewarding to me than adding columns of numbers every day."

Warren rounded the desk and placed his hands on her shoulders.

"Anna, you know that I am wealthy. I cannot deny that truth. But this—this place, this work, this is who I am. I don't care about money or wealth, and I especially don't care about the Florences of the world."

"I'm just a seamstress," she said softly.

"I'm just a newspaper editor," he said, searching her eyes.

Anna laughed. "You are far more than a newspaper editor."

"And you are far more than a seamstress. I have never known a woman with more inner strength of character than you. Every time we speak, I leave wanting to know more, to see you more. I know what I want in life, Anna. I want you. I want–I want to marry you."

"You–you what?"

Warren's cheeks and ears turned a bright shade of red. "I didn't mean for that to slip out, but yes, Anna, I want to marry you." His hands slid down her arms and he took her hands into his. "Listen, I know that society dictates certain practices, and I'm certain I will make many mistakes in that regard. The good Lord knows I've already blundered many times in my relationship with you so far. But I'm not that concerned with what society expects of me. I never have been. I don't want to spend years jumping through the hoops that others have set up for courting. I have watched my brother court Patricia for years and wondered why he didn't just marry her, start their life together, for goodness sake. And now look at him, on the verge of marriage and of a war he may never return from. I don't want that."

Warren paused. He lifted her hands and gently brushed his lips across both of her knuckles. "But I don't want to rush things, either. I do want to court you, Anna. I want you to understand how special I think you are. I want you to know that you deserve to be wooed in a way that you deserve. But I'm also not a patient man." He laughed and his cheeks reddened again. "I want you. I want to hold you in my arms. I want to show you off to the world, to tell everyone that you belong to me. I want the world to know that Miss Anna Drowne is mine, today and forever."

Anna just looked at him, eyes wide open. She would have convinced herself that she were standing in the middle of a dream had the all too real feel of Warren's hands not been causing her skin to warm under his touch.

"And I don't want to lose you again," he said, cupping her face in his hands. "These past couple of weeks have been the worst of my life."

For me as well," she whispered.

Her honest response brought another smile to his lips, a smile that faded slowly as his head dipped toward hers. Warren lightly brushed his lips against hers. "Promise me," he whispered. "Promise me that you'll never run from me again."

"I promise," she whispered back. "You have my word."

Warren captured her lips fully, sealing the promise with a kiss that let Anna know that this was, in fact, so very real.

13

REVELATIONS

"Why are you nervous?" Warren asked.

"Nervous? Don't be silly. What makes you think I'm nervous?"

"Because you continue to brush wrinkles from your skirt that aren't there. If you aren't careful, you'll wear the fabric completely away."

She hadn't realized she had been doing that, though she did notice how uncomfortable she had been since the cab dropped her off at the Mallory mansion thirty minutes ago. Folding her hands, Anna smirked at Warren. "I could ask you the same question, you know."

"What question?"

"Are you nervous?" she asked, smiling.

"Me? No. Why would I be?"

"I don't know, but the arm of your chair is wondering what it did to deserve the hole you are about to tap through it."

Warren made a fist and smiled a crooked grin. "Alright. Maybe a little nervous."

"Oh," she said, brushing again at the imaginary wrinkles of

her skirt. "You are worried that your father won't approve of me."

Warren's head snapped toward her. "What? No. That isn't it at all. I'm worried you won't approve of him."

"Why on Earth wouldn't I approve?"

"Well, my father is very, how do I say this… old money. And I know how you feel about old money."

Anna shook her head. "I'm sorry, Warren. I know my actions have given that impression, but really, I hold no ill feelings toward you or your father or anyone else of his standing."

"I'm glad to hear it. I don't want there to be anything else to come between us. Now, I've told, it's your turn. What has you so fidgety?"

She should tell him. This was a perfect time. They were alone. George had not returned from picking up Patricia for dinner and his father had not yet returned from his business trip. The deception had gone on long enough, and she didn't want to be introduced to the senior Mr. Mallory as Anna Drowne.

"Warren, I need to speak with you about something."

Warren stopped his tapping and turned in the seat to look at her. "Is everything alright?"

"I hope so," Anna began. "There is something I need to tell you. Something about me and my past."

Warren took her hand in his. "Don't look so grave. Nothing you could say will change how I feel about you."

I hope that's true, Anna thought. She breathed deeply, but before she could say another word, the front door was thrown open then slammed shut. A gentleman dressed in an overcoat and hat walked quickly past the drawing room before Anna could make out any of his features, save the salt and pepper facial hair he sported. The sound of another door slamming echoed through the hall.

The concerned look on Warren's face gave Anna pause. He squeezed her hand.

"Father knows nothing about you. His business trip

extended longer than expected, so he has been away for weeks. He wasn't trying to be rude. He just didn't know to stop and greet a guest before continuing to his study."

Anna watched Warren's face, his eyebrows still furrowed. "I didn't think him rude," she said.

"If you will excuse me," he said, smiling finally, "I'll let him know we have company."

Anna fiddled with the lace at her wrists while she waited for Warren's return. As she waited for him, she said a silent prayer that God would give her the strength she needed to tell Warren everything.

"You were about to tell him the truth. Am I correct, Miss Annabelle?"

Startled, Anna looked up and found Mr. Jameson standing in the doorway.

"I–I was, yes," she admitted.

"I am happy to hear that. It is time this all came to a resolution."

Anna wondered what he meant by 'all', but she had little time to wonder, because the front door flew open once more announcing the entrance of George and Patricia.

"Anna!" George said, taking her hand in greeting. "So good to see you again! Where is that knucklehead brother of mine?"

It was Mr. Jameson that answered. "Mr. Mallory has returned. Your brother is with him in the study. I believe your father will expect you to check in with him as well."

"Oh, certainly," George said, eyebrows furrowed just like his brother's. "Excuse me ladies. We'll be but a moment."

Winston Mallory closed the study door behind his sons and took his seat at his desk. He motioned for the boys to sit in the two leather chairs across from him.

"What have we done, father?" Warren laughed as he and his

brother approached the familiar chairs. "We haven't been summoned to these chairs since we were boys receiving a scolding for our latest scuffle."

"It isn't what you've done," the eldest Mallory said gravely. "It's what I'm about to do."

"Are you well?" George asked. "Your face is positively ashen."

"I'm not ill. Well, at least not physically. But I am sick at the choices I have made. Come. Sit. We have much to discuss."

"OH, PATRICIA, IT'S LOVELY!" Anna said.

"Thank you," Patricia said, admiring the diamond that now adorned her left ring finger. "Have you ever seen anything so beautiful?"

"No," Anna fibbed, smiling as she remembered the first time she herself had laid eyes on the beautiful engagement ring.

"Thirteen diamonds, one for every year he says he has been in love with me. Of course, that's absolutely ridiculous since we were mere children when we first met. But the thought is lovely, is it not?"

In love for thirteen years. Anna knew that feeling well. She smiled. "I think it is very sweet."

Patricia seemed to beam light itself as she sat in the chair across the table. Her cheeks flush, she looked every bit the woman in love, and Anna was very happy that she had made the decision all those weeks ago to return the ring to its rightful owner.

"That's unusual," Patricia said, looking out into the hall.

"What is?" Anna asked, following her gaze.

"This little impromptu meeting. It certainly isn't unusual for Mr. Mallory to drag George away for a discussion of the business, but I don't believe I have ever seen him include Warren."

"Warren told me that he is not an active member of the business."

"That's how George put it as well, but he did say he is still a financial partner. Something important must be happening to include Warren in the discussion. But, to be honest, I can't imagine anything so urgent that dinner has to be interrupted. Then again, I know very little of the automobile enterprise."

The entire city of Lansing had been built by money from the automobile industry, as far as Anna could see. That is probably what drew Anna's father here all those years ago as well.

Anna remembered Warren mentioning the automobile industry as well. "What exactly does their company do? Do they build cars?"

"Well, not cars, per se. They make wheels for cars, so obviously, they are very connected to the rest of the industry."

"A wheel company?" Anna said. She had a flashback to that day her father visited Warren's – the day they had argued. A feeling of dread began to creep over her skin. "What – what is the name of their company?"

"The Lansing Wheel Company. Have you heard of it?"

The room around Anna began to spin. She took several jagged breaths as the muscles tightened around her chest. The Lansing Wheel Company. Her father's company. Winston Mallory was the thief that stole her father's money. He was the one responsible for her mother's ruin.

She looked around the dining room of the Mallory mansion. She looked through the doors and into the hallway where a gilded framed mirror stared back at her. She remembered every detail of the drawing room she had visited over the past several weeks, every piece of art hanging in the hall. Every bit of opulence displayed in the mansion was purchased with the money earned from Henry Gibson's folly. Warren's wealth was due to Anna's impoverishment. A heaviness grew in her midsection and she felt the acids in her stomach roil.

"Anna? Are you feeling alright? You don't look well."

"I–I think I'm going to be sick. I need–I need some air," she said, rising from the table.

"Let me get my coat and I'll go for a walk with you."

"No!" Anna said a little too loudly. She took a deep breath. "No, I'll be fine. Stay here so the men won't wonder where we've gone."

Anna found her hat and bag by the front door. She fought back tears as she quickly fastened the hat, praying that she could make her exit before Warren and the other Mallory men came out of the study.

"May I be of assistance?" came a male voice from behind. She turned to find Mr. Jameson approaching her.

"I just need a little air," she said, reaching for the door.

"There are no cabs in the area this time of night."

Anna realized there was no point in lying to the eagle-eyed butler. "Would you please call one for me?"

"No."

Anna wasn't surprised. He was the Mallory's servant, and that is where his loyalties belonged. She reached for the door, praying God would provide a way home.

"There is no need to call a cab. Mr. Mallory's driver will take you home, Miss Annabelle."

WARREN WATCHED his younger brother as their father poured out his soul to his sons. So much of the story had already been shared with Warren, but this new revelation was a shock to both of the younger Mallorys.

"Why did you give up looking for her?" George asked.

"Her father-in-law led me to believe that she had returned home to England. When my man returned with no sign of her, we believed that she had remarried and was living under a new name. If that had been the case, it would have been nearly impossible to find her."

"And what makes you no longer believe that to be the case?"

"This," he said, holding out his hand to reveal a flower-shaped, Austrian crystal brooch. "I found it in the window of a pawn shop on Capitol Avenue. The shop owner said that he thought it was stolen at first, but the woman, who he described as a beauty with an English accent, insisted that it was hers. He said she needed it to pay her rent, claimed it was the last piece of jewelry she owned."

"It's beautiful," George said, taking it from his father and turning it over in his hand. "But how do you know for certain it belongs to her."

Winston rubbed his temples. "The inscription on the back."

"*Forever, W.M.* Those are your initials."

"Yes. The brooch was a gift from me."

Warren breathed deeply and leaned back in his chair. "How much of the business is hers?"

"Half of it."

"Half?" George said, leaning back in his chair as well.

Warren watched a myriad of emotions play across his brother's face. Losing half of the family business would impact Warren financially, but he also had his investment in the newspaper to fall back on. George, as the chief operating officer of Lansing Wheel, was far more affected by the news.

"Well," George began, "I suppose we will need to take out a loan if she wants a full cash payout, but I don't see a problem making those arrangements. However, if she wishes to remain a silent partner, I can have Higgins draw up a trust that would pay out quarterly, or monthly, if she wishes. Silent partnership is a better choice, in my opinion. She'll have to invest an amount that large anyway, she might as well keep it where it is and benefit from the growth our company is undergoing."

Winston Mallory eyed his youngest son thoughtfully. "You aren't upset?"

"Upset? Why would I be upset?"

"Most men would be upon hearing that half of their fortune belonged to someone else."

"The half that remains ours is still a fairly hefty amount, father, and Lansing Wheel isn't the only company we own. It's the most profitable, yes, but we have a fortune built in our other investments as well. Regardless, if the money belongs to another, then it is our duty to return it. Especially now that we know the dire circumstances the woman is under."

"The only problem that remains is finding her. I've tried unsuccessfully in the past."

"Yes," Warren said, "but you weren't looking in the right place. You looked in Pennsylvania and in England, but did you ever look right here in Lansing?"

"No, because she had disappeared completely from society. I assumed that meant she had left the area."

"Well, then first thing tomorrow our search begins." Warren moved to his father's side and clasped his shoulder. "And, as luck would have it, I have become very good at locating missing women."

"What is that supposed to mean?"

"He can explain it over dinner. I'm famished," George said, rising as well. "Let's join the women in the dining room. Patricia and I have an announcement to make. Plus, I believe my big brother has someone very special he would like you to meet."

"Yes." Warren smiled. "That is, if she hasn't disappeared while you've sequestered us in here!"

14

CONFESSIONS

*E*lizabeth Gibson slowly removed the pins from her daughter's hair. Sobs shook the young woman's body so violently that the task was rather difficult, but it gave the mother something to do while she waited for the crying to subside.

Elizabeth had been waiting for this moment. It had been two weeks since Anna had been fired and her world turned upside down, but not once had she broken down. Elizabeth, always a strong woman herself, had volleyed between being proud of her daughter's inner strength, so like her own, and being concerned that Anna was bottling too many emotions inside. Obviously, her inner turmoil, mixed with the stress of completing all the dress work she had taken on over the past few weeks, had finally gotten the best of her.

Elizabeth ran her fingers through the amber-colored locks, working out the pompadour Anna had worked so diligently on this morning, laying ringlets across her shoulders. When Anna calmed somewhat, Elizabeth took the opportunity to speak.

"My dearest, are you ready to talk to me?" Her daughter sat up slightly, and wiped her face with the handkerchief Elizabeth offered.

"Oh, Mumma," she said, using the term of endearment she hadn't spoken in years. "I've been a fool. Such a fool." She collapsed back onto her mother's lap and began sobbing again.

Elizabeth returned to the task of smoothing out the knots in Anna's hair and waited for her to calm again.

"Better to consider yourself a fool than a sage. 'Seest thou a man wise in his own conceit? There is more hope of a fool than him.'" she said, lifting Anna's chin. "Come, moppet, things aren't always as bad as we think. It usually helps to talk about it."

"I don't even know where to begin."

"How about the beginning?" her mother smiled.

"The beginning? Well, I guess that means I have to start at the theater—"

"The theater?" Elizabeth interrupted. How many weeks had passed since they had attended that play? "Alright, love, if that is where your story begins…I'm listening."

Anna sat up on the bed. "Something happened that night. Do you remember when you left to get some air?"

Elizabeth remembered well. She remembered the crowded foyer. She remembered seeing him across the room, almost certain that he had seen her. She remembered the look on his face, the determination in his eyes as he began weaving through the crowd toward her. She remembered slipping quickly out the side door and circling the building, before hiding in a side alley until she was certain the intermission had ended. "Yes, I remember."

"While you were gone, a man visited our box."

Elizabeth flinched. "The gentleman from across the theater?" she asked anxiously.

"No, well not the one you are thinking of. It was a younger man. He thought I was staring at him. He began flirting with me."

"Oh, I see." Elizabeth smiled. So, Anna's tears weren't about her change in circumstance. They were about a man.

"No, mother, you don't see. The man was Warren."

"Warren? Warren who–" But even as the question left her lips, Elizabeth remembered. Warren Mallory. She rose from the bed and walked toward the window. "The Mallory boy. And you are certain? It has been an awfully long time, and you were so little."

"There is no doubt."

Elizabeth turned back to her daughter. "Anna, why are you crying over a run-in with a gentleman that happened weeks ago?"

"Because," Anna said, tears spilling once again down her cheeks. "He has been courting me."

"Courting you?" Elizabeth gripped the dining chair. "I don't understand."

"I knew you wouldn't approve," Anna said, shaking her head and staring at her hands as they tugged at the handkerchief, twisting it around her finger. "I knew how you felt about the life we once lived. Warren is a part of that past."

"Do you understand how much of our past is connected to the Mallorys?" Elizabeth asked, staring at Anna. How could she tell her daughter? How much should she reveal?

"Yes."

"Yes? Yet you continued to see him? How could you, knowing what his father has done?"

Anna looked up at her mother. "But, I didn't know. Not until tonight. I only learned tonight, while dining at their home…"

"You were at the Mallory mansion?"

Anna only nodded.

"Was this the first time?"

Anna shook her head.

"I see," Elizabeth said, remembering her visit from Mr. Jameson. "So, that is what he meant when he said he had seen you."

"Who?"

"Jameson."

"The butler? You've spoken with their butler?"

"Yes. He visited me a couple of weeks ago."

"How…how did he find you?"

"I'm not exactly certain, but he mentioned seeing you and he knew that we both worked for Mrs. Trudy."

Anna's forehead wrinkled. "If he knows where we live, Warren could show up any moment. I can't see him, Mother. I couldn't bear it," she said, falling face down on the bed in another wave of sobbing.

"No, I don't think he will. If Mr. Jameson hasn't exposed us yet, I don't believe he will."

"Why wouldn't he?"

"Because, he seems to still hold some loyalty toward me."

"Loyalty? Why would the Mallory butler be loyal to you?"

"Because, he used to be my butler. When your grandpapa grew ill and I discovered that the estate was bankrupt, it became clear that I had to marry a man of means. Your father had already expressed an interest in me when he had visited London for business. Once the arrangements were made, Mr. Jameson offered to escort me to America. He would soon be out of a job, anyway. Since your father already had a full staff, I helped him procure work with the Mallorys when we arrived stateside."

"You helped him? You knew the Mallorys before you came to America?"

Elizabeth sighed. "Yes. I had met Mr. and Mrs. Mallory when I was young, while I still lived in England."

"So, you were friends with Warren's mother?"

"I might have been, had she not passed away before I moved to America. I married your father, but kept some contact with Mr. Mallory, out of memory of his wife. I was the one that actually introduced your father to him."

"And that's how they became business partners?"

"They were never partners, though your father tried."

"I don't understand."

"We spent a great deal of time with Winston Mallory. He

seemed to enjoy our company, and we became great friends. But then, it became obvious that our friendship, that is, the friendship between me and Mr. Mallory, became more than it should."

Anna was listening intently, but the pained look of shock on her face nearly broke Elizabeth.

"Nothing ever happened, you need to believe that, Anna. Your father and I did not marry out of love, but we did hold an affection for one another, mostly because we shared you. But even without love, our marriage commitment was solid. I would never betray the vow I made to God and your father. Marriage is sacred. You believe me, don't you?"

"Yes," Anna said, her voice wavering.

"But Winst–Mr. Mallory and I grew close. I felt myself falling in love with him, and I know he felt the same. We both knew it was wrong, so we cut off all communication between us. I thought he was settled with it, but he refused to do any business dealings with your father after that."

"Then how did he come to own Lansing Wheel?"

"Your father's body wasn't even cold before Winston Mallory swooped in and bought up the company. He probably purchased it for far less than it was worth, since the company could not survive without your father's business sense."

"So, he is the one who refused to repay father's loan?"

"It was the previous owners, then Mr. Mallory purchased the company. Under new ownership, all past loans were made void. I knew I had little chance of regaining your father's money with the original men, but under a new owner, it would have been impossible."

"And…you never heard from him again?"

"I never heard from him again. That's why I was so surprised when Mr. Jameson appeared on our doorstep. I thought Winston had sent him, but now I'm not so certain."

"So, you were in love with Warren's father?"

"It's a very long story, darling, for another time," Elizabeth said, returning to the bed and stroking her daughter's hair. "Tonight's story is about you. Why would Warren Mallory seek you out tonight?"

Anna poured out her story. Like a stressed levee that has finally broke, every detail of the last month gushed from her with abandon. She left no detail out, even the most intimate moments she and Warren had shared. When she had finished, she looked at her mother with anxious eyes. Elizabeth Gibson said nothing. After several silent moments, Anna asked, "Mother, are you angry?"

"No," she said as she wiped her silent tears from her cheeks. "Only hurt."

"Oh, Mumma, I'm so sorry. This is why I didn't tell you before. I knew you would be hurt by my actions. I know how you feel about my discontent with our little life."

"I'm not hurt by that," Elizabeth said, still stroking Anna's hair. "I'm hurt that you felt you couldn't tell me. I've never known you to keep secrets from me. It feels as if I lost a part of you these past months."

"No, oh no, Mother. I'm still here. I'm still the same Anna. I'm so sorry I've made you feel that way."

"No, it is I that should apologize to you. In my attempt to shelter you from the evils of this world, I instead put up a wall between us that you felt unable to climb. I should have been there for you."

"But don't you see? You were right. It was me. I was the one in the wrong. Had I listened to your advice, had I turned Warren away from the beginning, I wouldn't be hurting now."

"But if you had felt able to come to me earlier, I could have told you about Warren's father. I could have saved you this heartache."

"I'm not certain you could have, mother," Anna said, grabbing her mother's hands. "I think it took this final blow for me to see what I couldn't before."

"What do you see now?"

"What you tried telling me all those weeks ago, that night after the play. You spoke of discontent and God's Will, but I didn't understand. Yes, I understood your pain, and I agreed with what you were saying because I didn't want you to hurt for another second. But I didn't fully understand what I understand now."

"And what is that?"

"That I have spent far too much of my life living in discontent, without realizing it. I have spent thirteen years pining for a boy that I met a couple of times. I had made him into this fantasy, an unrealistic ideal that no real-life man could hold up to. Then, when that man did come back into my life, I refused to see that he wasn't that fantasy man, that I couldn't make the invention into a reality. It took this final blow for me to see what you, and God, have been saying all along. I can't keep running after things that aren't God's plan for me."

"Anna, I should never have led you to believe that God's plan couldn't include a man of means."

"The point is, it has to be God's plan, not mine, not Warren's. God's. I have spent no time asking God for his guidance in this situation. Why is that? Because I was afraid of what He would say. But I'm not afraid anymore. When Mrs. Trudy fired me, I fell at God's feet, and look what He was able to do? I am making more money doing what I love, not just sewing, but designing original pieces. It took God taking away what I clung to – the job, and the financial stability that came with it – before he could give me what he wanted me to have. And His plan is so much more than I could have done on my own."

"Just like Gertrude," her mother smiled.

"Gertrude?" Anna said, wiping her tears and looking at her mother. "What has she got to do with anything?"

Elizabeth laughed and rose to retrieve the doll from the shelf. "Do you remember how upset you were with your father?"

"I cried for days."

"Yes, and do you remember how angry you were with me when I told you it was time to stop mourning?"

Anna blushed. "I didn't know you could tell that I was upset with you."

"Oh, yes!" Elizabeth laughed again. "You wouldn't sit in my lap or look me in the eye. Do you remember what I said to you that morning before Warren returned your doll?"

Anna thought a moment. "Vaguely. I do remember being held in your arms and comforted."

"I told you that sometimes we have to give up what we hold most dear so God can give us something bigger. I told you about my sadness over leaving my home, leaving England. But then God gave you to me so quickly after marrying your father, and I knew that God's plan was bigger than my own."

"And Gertrude was like that?"

"Yes." Elizabeth handed the doll to Anna. "You and I prayed together that morning that God would help you give up Gertrude, that you would forgive your father and respect his decision, because it was the right thing to do."

"Wait, I think I do remember this part. I remember feeling so much better after that prayer."

"Yes, and then, within hours, you not only had Gertrude back, but with a beautiful new dress as well."

"So, he gave me back what I wanted most," Anna said, running a finger along the ruffles of the pale green dress.

"Yes, but only when you were willing to do it His way."

"Mother? Would you pray with me again? That I could give this all up…Warren, the desire to be wealthy again, all of it? I truly want to desire nothing in my life that isn't God's will for me."

As the women knelt side by side and prayed for God to mend Anna's heart and help her to move on, another prayer was being sent heavenward on the other side of Lansing that petitioned God to do exactly the opposite.

GIVING UP AND MOVING ON

The heavy, carved door closed in a resounding thud as it slammed into the door jamb. Warren strode straight to the drawing room, throwing his coat and hat onto his mother's chair. His hand snatched another upholstered chair as he walked by it, dragging it loudly across the floor of the room. He positioned the chair in front of the large window that faced the street and threw himself into it. A streak of muddy water made a path down the wall as he kicked up his feet to rest on the windowsill.

It was time to give up. He should have given up days ago, but he just couldn't. He wanted—no, needed—to see her, talk to her. But she was nowhere to be found. He had no other choice now but to face the truth. Anna had disappeared again, and this time, he wasn't going to be able to find her.

"Isn't it strange, that after years of searching the globe, Mrs. Gibson was right here in Lansing, right under your father's nose."

Warren didn't take his eyes off the rain that slid down the panes of the window. After all these years, the butler's stealth entrances no longer caught him off guard. Somewhere in the recesses of his mind, Warren always expected the man to be somewhere close by.

"If only he had looked closer," the butler continued, despite Warren's lack of response.

"Maybe it wouldn't have mattered," Warren said, realizing the man wasn't going to leave. "Maybe she didn't want to be found."

"I find it impossible to believe that any woman who is lost wouldn't want to be found."

"All I know is that I now understand why my father gave up looking for Mrs. Gibson. It is excruciating to search for a woman that does not want to be found."

"Are we still discussing Elizabeth Gibson?" the butler asked, eyebrows raised.

Warren finally turned sleep deprived eyes toward the butler. "I should have admitted to myself that it was over when she didn't return from her walk that night. But I thought, well, if she was ill, it would take a couple of days to get better. After a week with no word, a smart man would have realized that she wanted nothing to do with him. But, apparently, I'm not a smart man."

"I take it your visit with Miss Leonne did not go well."

Warren grunted. "She said she doesn't know where Anna lives, but I'm not sure I believe her. I left a message for Anna, but the look on her face told me not to hold my breath."

"So, you are giving up?"

"She promised me she wouldn't run again, but that is exactly what she did."

"Promised? Well, that seems rather unrealistic, now doesn't it, sir."

"What does that mean?" Warren snapped.

"How can a woman promise not to run when she doesn't yet know what she is running from?"

"Well, if she doesn't know, then I'm more confused than ever, because I am certain I have no idea why she keeps disappearing."

"I didn't say she didn't know why she was running at the time of her departure. I'm suggesting she didn't know at the time of the promise, thus making it an unrealistic oath."

Warren rubbed his temples. "You aren't making any sense. A promise is a promise. If a woman can't keep her word, how can I trust her."

"Oh, now trust. Trust is another matter all together. I believe that trust, or lack there of, is a topic worth investigating with the young woman."

"I will not be discussing trust, or any other topic for that matter, with the young woman. She has disappeared. She doesn't want to be found. It's time I face the truth."

"Facing the truth would settle this entire issue, if you ask me."

Warren squinted. "Honestly, I can't tell if you are agreeing with me or patronizing me."

"I never patronize," Mr. Jameson said. "But I seldom agree with you."

Warren turned back to face the rain sliding down the foggy window, hoping the Butler would leave as quietly as he had entered. It had been a long week, and Warren just wished for some solitude to clear his mind. Either Jameson was unable to read Warren's thoughts, or unwilling to.

"I wonder what would have happened if your father hadn't given up all those years ago."

"What other choice did he have?" Warren answered without turning. "He had nowhere else to search."

"Didn't he? I believe receiving news that she had likely married another man did help him in making the decision to quit his search."

Warren thought about what his father had told him about coveting Henry Gibson's wife. A broken heart might very well have led him to stop his search. Was the same thing happening to Warren?

"I don't know what else I can do," Warren said softly, turning back to the window.

"You could stop acting like your father."

The chair scraped loudly against the grain of the wood floor as Warren jerked to his feet. "What is that supposed to mean?"

"You've looked far and wide to no avail, so you are giving up. Maybe if you look closer."

"Closer? Are you suggesting there are clues nearby?"

"Closer than you think."

Warren eyed the servant suspiciously. What kind of game was the man playing? He was hesitant, but decided to play along anyway. "Alright, Mr. Jameson. If you were to search for a woman who did not want to be found, where would you begin?"

A slow smile spread across the man's face. "Well, sir, since you have asked, I would say that I would begin by speaking with Barney."

"The driver?"

"Yes. It would seem to me that he might remember exactly where he dropped her off the other evening."

"Blast it, Jameson! Why didn't you tell me our driver took her home?"

"You didn't ask," he answered simply. "I cannot answer that which is not asked."

Warren stared blankly at the man. The muscles in his shoulders tightened. He could feel anger rising in his chest, but he wasn't certain if he was angry with the butler or himself. Then realization dawned. He was angry, yes, but not with Mr. Jameson. He was angry with Anna.

Warren stuffed his fists into his pants pockets and walked towards the door. "I'll be in my room if anyone needs me."

"Sir?"

Warren sighed. "She knows where to find me. I'm done chasing her."

"As you wish," Mr. Jameson said. "But I do hope the future

does not find you scanning the windows of pawn shops looking for a sign of something long lost."

Warren stopped at the bottom of the stairs.

"Do you really think she wants to be found?"

"I think she doesn't realize she is lost."

Lost. There was a time in Warren's life when he was lost and didn't realize it. But like the parable of the lost sheep, God never gave up pursuing him until he was found. Warren was lost and broken, but Jesus shouldered his sin and carried him home. But Anna wasn't lost, not the way that Warren had been lost. And Warren certainly didn't have the relentless patience of God.

He continued up the stairs, hoping his room would afford him refuge from the intrusive servant, if not from his own tortured thoughts.

~

"He's been here twice, you know," Charlotte said, lifting her arms.

Anna continued pinning the seam under Miss Leonne's arm, but she said nothing.

"He left you a note this time," Charlotte said.

"That ought to take care of that loose bodice," Anna said, rising from her knees. "Let's try the green dress next. I'm afraid that bodice is going to have the same problem as this one."

Charlotte turned to face Anna. "So, is this how it's going to be? First, you ignore him, and now you are going to ignore me?"

"I'm not ignoring you, I just do not wish to discuss it."

"Anna, you may not think that this is any of my business, but he continues to show up here and ask me questions. Don't you think I deserve some sort of an explanation?"

"There is nothing to explain. I just don't want to see him anymore."

"What did this man do to make you end the relationship so abruptly?"

"Nothing."

"Nothing? Surely there's more to the story than that?"

Anna laid the straight pins on the table and began unbuttoning the back of the dress.

"You know, you won't be able to hide from him forever," Charlotte said as she stepped from the gown. "Lansing is not that large of a town."

"I know. I have thought of that."

Anna helped Charlotte into the shimmery, pale green evening gown. Charlotte sighed as she looked at her reflection.

"This one is lovely. You have outdone yourself."

Anna smiled at Charlotte. "This was actually inspired by a doll's dress." She hadn't realized it until now, but as she let the layers of soft green fabric slide between her fingers, she knew without a doubt that she had been thinking of Warren when she designed this gown. She thought of him constantly and wondered if every piece she fashioned in the future would have some sort of reflection of a memory of the man.

"I may have a solution," Charlotte said, twirling to face Anna and breaking her from her daydream. "Come with me to New York."

"New York?"

"I've just been offered the lead in a Broadway musical," Charlotte said, squeezing both of Anna shoulders. "You can come with me. I know a lot of people in the fashion world in New York City. With your talent and the right introductions, I know that your career as a designer will flourish in the city."

"But—what about my mother?"

"Bring her! Couldn't we all do with a change of scenery?"

Anna was uncertain she could ever convince her mother, but the idea of moving to New York intrigued her. A new home, a new life, a new career, all without the fear of running into Warren.

"I'll think about it," Anna said.

"Truly?"

"I'm not making any promises other than that I'll think about it."

"Oh, Anna! What a grand adventure we will have!"

As Charlotte continued blathering on about the theaters and shops and social life of New York City, Anna found her mood actually lifting. She had felt trapped under a heavy blanket of depression ever since she left the Mallory Mansion for the last time. Maybe the adventure that Charlotte proposed might actually be the balm Anna needed to sooth her aching heart.

But why, then, did her heart feel so heavy at the thought of leaving Lansing?

UNPACKING THE TRUTH

*A*nna latched her suitcase closed for what she hoped to be the last time. She had spent the last half an hour circling the apartment, looking for items she couldn't do without, packing them, then deciding that she could in fact do without them. She unpacked the items and began the search once again. After several rounds of this ridiculous game, Anna decided she had had enough. If she left anything behind worthwhile, she could have her mother send it or she could purchase a new one. She had no doubt that the stores in New York offered every bit the variety that she could find here in Lansing, most likely more.

"I've left the majority of the money I've earned the last several weeks in the cookie jar. There is enough to sustain you for a few months, but if Charlotte is correct about my future as a designer, I'll be sending you more money very soon."

"I'm sure I'll manage," her mother said quietly. "I hope to reduce my bills somewhat once you are gone."

"Oh?" Anna said, folding a few extra handkerchiefs for her handbag.

"I've spoken with Mrs. Caffey from church."

"Will's mother?"

"Yes. With William serving in the Great War, she has extra room in her home. She said I could rent a room from her."

"That is fantastic," Anna said, turning toward her mother. "I won't worry about you half as much knowing that you won't be alone."

"You needn't worry about me, dear. I will survive. God has always seen to that," she said, picking up her hat.

"Are you going somewhere? Esther and her father will be here soon."

"I thought I would take a walk in the park." Her mother gave a weak smile. "If it wouldn't hurt you too much, I believe it will be easier for me to say goodbye now, rather than watch as all of your luggage is carried out. I don't think I will be able to hold myself together at that point."

"You mustn't be too emotional," Anna said, swallowing the lump in her own throat. "New York isn't so very far away. And I will come back to visit…and you will come visit me, won't you?"

Her mother reached for Anna's hand. "We shall see," she said, tears glistening in her eyes. "Now give me a squeeze, before I lose the strength to let you go."

Anna choked on her next breath as a sob that she couldn't control found its way to the top of her throat. She nearly threw herself into her mother's arms.

"Oh, Mumma! I will miss you so."

"And I will miss you too, my darling. Are you certain this is the right decision?"

"You know it is my only choice. I can't stay here, not knowing that he is so close."

Her mother pulled back and cradled Anna's tear-stained face in her hands. "But you won't be able to run from the memories. Trust me. I know."

"I have to try," was all she could say.

Elizabeth wrapped her arms around Anna one last time,

kissed her cheek and opened the door. She stopped and turned to look one last time.

"I'm praying for you, Annabelle. I'm praying for God's protection as you search for His will in your life." And with that, she shut the door and was gone.

After several moments of uninhibited crying, Anna lifted her eyes.

"Lord, this hurts so much," she prayed. "Please help me."

Anna raised her head and her eyes settled on her Bible. With all of her pacing and fretting, how had she missed packing her most precious possession? She picked it up and sat down at the small table. When she opened it, the pages fell open to Joshua 1:9.

"Be strong and courageous," Anna read aloud. "Do not be frightened, and do not be dismayed, for the Lord your God is with you wherever you go."

A quiet calm fall over her as she reread the scripture. God was with her, no matter where she traveled. She would be leaving her mother, but God would still be with her.

After spending a few more minutes in prayer, Anna felt surprisingly refreshed. Her tears ceased just as Esther and her father knocked at her door.

"The door is open," Anna yelled over her shoulder. She struggled to pack her Bible in her already overstuffed valise. "You can take those bags by the door, if you like. I only have this one last item to attend to."

"And where exactly would you like me to take them?"

Anna whipped around to face the voice, Bible still clutched to her chest.

"Warren," she said, barely above a whisper. Seeing him there, standing in the middle of her apartment, made it difficult to breathe, let alone speak.

He removed his hat and threw it on the table before unbuttoning his coat and stuffing his hands into his pants pockets. His eyes never left Anna. He was as handsome as ever, Anna thought, but something was different. He seemed strange, unlike she had ever seen him.

"Going somewhere?" he asked sharply.

Anger. That is what was different about him. He was angry, and she was certain she knew why. He was angry with her, and although she knew he had every right to be, something inside of her broke seeing him like this.

Anna's insides quivered. A deep ache rose in her chest and she knew that if she didn't escape the situation quickly, she would do something foolish like begin to cry or, worse yet, throw herself into his arms and ask for forgiveness. But she couldn't push past him and run away, unless she were able to grab all of her baggage on her departure. That was impossible. No, she couldn't leave. Somehow, she had to make him leave. She had to use his anger to her advantage.

"Yes. I'm moving," she said, attempting to sound as haughty as possible. "I feel I am in need of a new beginning."

"Is that so?" he asked, unscathed by her attitude. "What's the matter? Lansing no longer to your liking?"

"Lansing is perfectly fine. It's its inhabitants that I have tired of."

Warren threw his head back and laughed, and Anna bit her bottom lip in frustration. How was she going to get him to storm out of her apartment if he was going to laugh every time she attempted to say something mean. She decided to try a more direct approach.

"You need to leave. My ride will be here any moment."

"I'll leave when I'm ready," he said, casually strolling to the window. He picked up a book that her mother had left on the windowsill and thumbed through the pages. The breeze through the open window ruffled his brown hair out of place.

"Where are you headed?" he asked without looking up.

"New York." Why had she told him that? Did she want him following after her? Yes, she realized. Of course, she wanted him to follow after her.

Warren looked at her, eyebrows raised. "The Big Apple, eh? What is enticing you to that part of the country?"

Anna couldn't take the ill-tempered way he looked at her. She knew she couldn't be with him, but it was killing her to see the face that always held such gaity look at her with such hatred.

"Why–why are you here, Warren?"

"Why am I here? Closure," he said, snapping the book closed. "Or something like that, though I'm not certain why. You seemed to have moved on quite swiftly. I suppose I should do the same."

I'm trying to move on, her heart screamed, but her lips stayed silent. She watched as he replaced the book on the windowsill and turned his back on her to peruse her mother's small collection of books.

He took another book off the shelf. "Why?" he asked, void of all emotion.

"Why am I leaving?"

"That's not what I meant."

I know, her heart screamed. "I couldn't continue a lie."

The words slipped out before she knew they were in her mouth. They were true. She couldn't keep lying to him about her identity, yet she couldn't tell him the truth knowing who his father was and how he had destroyed her mother.

"A lie?" he said, turning slowly. "What lie? The lie you told me when you promised you wouldn't run again? Or was our entire relationship a lie?" He slammed the book down on the table. "Please, Anna, tell me the truth, once and for all, or are you incapable of the task?"

Her heart shattered into a million pieces. His words stung so deeply, as he had most certainly intended, and it took everything in her to hold back the tears.

"Leave!" she managed to squeak out. "I never want to see you again."

"Gladly," he said, reaching for his hat. He grabbed the book off the table and turned to replace it on the shelf. His back was to her, but something about his demeanor changed. His shoulders, only seconds earlier a solid, tense block, relaxed somewhat. What was he looking at...

Anna gripped the chair to steady herself. It wasn't possible that he recognized her, was it? But even as she wondered, Warren reached up and took Gertrude down from her place on the shelf.

"This is a beautiful doll," he remarked, running a finger down the side of Gertrude's face. "Where did you get it?"

"My–my father bought it for me."

"It looks very expensive."

"I wouldn't know," she said honestly. She truly had no idea how much her father had paid for the doll.

"And the dress?" he asked, peering at Anna over his shoulder. "Is this the original garment?"

"It–it has been so long. I was just a child."

"That's not really an answer, now is it? Are you saying that you don't know, or are you avoiding my question?" he said, raising one eyebrow.

Silence was the only answer she offered. Their eyes locked, hazel piercing amber, and neither of them breathed.

"Where did the dress come from, Anna?"

Her fingers dug into the upholstery as she struggled to steady herself. She had to get rid of him. He couldn't find out the truth. Not now, not when she was so close to leaving all of this behind.

"I'm not–I'm not really certain. It could have been purchased at Arbaugh's Department Store."

"We both know that it was not," he said. He begun to untie the back of the doll's dress.

"Stop!" Anna said. "What are you doing?"

Warren did not stop until he had removed the dress.

"Please, Warren, you mustn't," she said weakly, but it was too late. He had turned the dress inside out and was reading the words embroidered in the back.

"To Princess Grace," he sighed. He stood with the dress in one hand, Gertrude in the other, forehead knit in confusion. Anna held her breath as he slowly lifted his gaze to hers.

"Princess Grace?" he asked. But even as the words left his mouth, he squeezed his eyes shut and grimaced. "Annabelle Grace. I remember. Oh, how could I be so stupid."

The tears fell freely down her cheeks now as Warren threw both the doll and the dress on the chair and grabbed her by the shoulders.

"You. You are Annabelle."

She was finding it difficult to breathe, let alone answer him. The best she could offer was a slight nod and more sobbing.

"But why? Why didn't you tell me?"

"I–I wanted to," she said when she could finally find her voice.

"How long have you known? When did you realize I was, well, me?"

Amber pools locked onto him. "Since the first moment I looked at you."

"At the theater? And you said nothing?"

"What should I have said? Hello there, you don't remember me, but I have been in love with you since I was nine years old."

Eyes wide, Warren tightened his grip. "What did you just say?"

She bit her lip and shook her head. She had already said too much.

"Anna, you said you were in love with me. Is that true?" When she still refused to answer, he released his grip on her shoulders to cradle her face in his hands. "I demand an answer. Either you love me or you don't, but I won't leave here until you say the words."

Her skin tingled beneath his touch. "Please don't make me say it," she whispered. "It hurts too much."

Warren exhaled deeply as a smile slid across his handsome

face. But the look was soon replaced with confusion. "Why did you run away? Why did you leave me?"

She shook her head. "Because we can never be."

"I've told you before. I don't care about your circumstances."

"There's so much more you don't know," her voice cracked. "My past…our pasts have crossed in a way that makes it impossible. Your father has done things that–"

"My father?"

"I know you don't understand, but my mother–"

"Your mother?" he interrupted her. He threw back his head and squeezed his eyes tight. "My father and your mother. Oh, Anna," he said looking at her. "I understand far more than you realize."

"Then you must see that I cannot, no, I will not hurt my mother further. She has endured enough. How can we be together? It would be a daily reminder of what your father has done."

"I know exactly what my father has done," Warren said, reaching for her hand and pulling her behind him. He grabbed his hat and headed for the door.

"Where are you taking me?"

"To the one person that can solve this mystery, once and for all."

THE SEARCH IS OVER

*A*fter so many bleak and dreary days of rain, the beautiful sunny day brought everything in the park to life. Tall, proud irises opened their sleepy heads while squirrels ran up and down the tree next to the bench on which Elizabeth sat. One particular squirrel came surprisingly close, eyeing Elizabeth for any sign of treats that she may have to share with him. She shooed him away, not wanting to be bothered. Normally, the critter would have brought a smile to her face. But try as she might, she couldn't bring herself to enjoy any beauty the Lord had made today.

How had life gotten so discombobulated? Her heart wrenched at the thought of what she had done to her daughter. In her attempt to protect her from the harm and the pain that she herself had faced in life, she had brought more pain and heartache to her than she had ever wished. When Anna had first told her about Charlotte Leonne's offer to travel with her to New York, Elizabeth had tried to convince her daughter not to go. She knew better than anyone that Anna was only running from her problems. Anna insisted that it was what she wanted, that it was a new start to a new future for herself. But Elizabeth knew if she had never discouraged Anna, if she had never told her the truth about Warren's father, Anna would most likely be happily settling in to a relationship with the boy she had been in love with her entire life. But no matter how hard she tried, Elizabeth could not convince Anna differently.

Who was to blame for Elizabeth Gibson's troubles? There were so many factors that led to her ruin. She could blame Henry for not having the good sense to have a will in place for his family, or the senior Mr. Gibson, whose cold heart and self-ishness certainly contributed to her situation. Maybe she should be angry with her father for mismanaging the remainder of the estate before his death. And what of God? Isn't He the one that holds her life in his hands? Hadn't he promised to prosper her, and not to harm her? But of all these factors, there was only one person Elizabeth felt malice toward – Winston Mallory. And she had allowed that malice to not only eat away at her heart all of these years, she was now allowing it to push away the only thing Elizabeth had left, her precious Anna. She couldn't let that happen.

Elizabeth grabbed her handbag and was just rising when a black Oldsmobile pulled up alongside of the park. A man stepped out and reached in to assist a young woman out of the vehicle. She recognized the dress of the woman before she even saw the anxious face above it. Anna made her way toward her mother, the finely dressed gentleman at her side. Warren, Elizabeth presumed. Why were they here? And together? What had transpired in the hour Elizabeth had been in the park?

She was so preoccupied with the couple approaching her and what their presence indicated that she didn't immediately notice the other gentleman that stepped out of the car as well. Anna and Warren met Elizabeth in front of the bench.

"What is the meaning of this?" her mother said, an uncertain smile breaking across her face. As she spoke, the other gentleman stepped up and joined the party. He removed his hat and Elizabeth's smile quickly disappeared.

Forgiveness. The word rang in her ears as loudly as if she had spoken the word herself. It was the Lord speaking to her, but she wasn't certain she was able, or willing, to obey.

"You?" Elizabeth spat. Her heart raced and even the pain caused by her own nails digging into the palms of her hands did little to keep her eyes from moistening. She clenched her jaw, refusing to let the man see her tears. Not after all these years.

"Mother, forgive me."

Elizabeth turned to her daughter and found that she was making no effort to stop the tears that fell down her cheeks. She reached out and wiped Anna's face.

"My precious, dear Annabelle. What have you to be sorry for? It is I who should apologize to you. I should never have let my bitterness come between you and the one you love."

Winston took a step closer to her. "Beth—"

"No," Elizabeth interrupted. She turned her attention back to the elder Mallory. "No, Mr. Mallory, do not confuse my affection for my daughter as an invitation for you to address me. I am willing to accept your son into my daughter's life, but I will never accept you. Ever."

"Please, Mother. You must listen to him."

"Anna, you have no idea what you are asking of me."

Forgiveness. Elizabeth shook her head.

"Please trust me," Anna said.

"Elizabeth," he said, taking another step. "I've been a fool."

"That is an understatement," Elizabeth hissed.

Winston looked down at the hat he twisted in his hands. "If I could go back, I would do everything differently."

"By everything, are you referring to the stealing of my husband's fortune?"

"I stole nothing from Henry."

"No, you waited until he was dead so you could steal it from me."

"Not true. I waited the customary eighteen months that I knew you would expect any gentleman to observe before I came to call on you, but when I did, I found no sign of you or your daughter."

"Eighteen months! You purchased the company days after the passing of my husband, yet you waited eighteen months to speak with me?"

"I was waiting for your mourning period to end."

"Business matters need not be governed by mourning practices."

"I was hoping to offer you more than a business proposition, Elizabeth."

Elizabeth breathed in sharply. Winston stepped closer.

"I hired an investigator. He tracked down your former father-in-law. The investigator told him I was looking for you, told him I had financial business to discuss with you. Henry's father led my man to believe that you and the child returned to your family in England."

"A wild goose chase," Elizabeth said. "Thomas Gibson is well aware of the fact that my father died penniless. There was nothing for me to return to."

"I had no idea," Winston said. "Oh, Beth, you must believe me. I sent my man to England to look for you. After months and months with no leads, he convinced me that you had likely remarried and that with a change of name, it would be impossible to find you. The thought of you, once again, married to another man, it broke me. Regardless of that heart-break, I have sent the same investigator to England every year to look for new evidence. But, as you can imagine, to no avail."

"You expect me to believe that you have spent the last dozen years searching the globe for me? Why on earth would you do that?"

"Let's not pretend that you don't know how I felt about you…how I still feel about you."

Elizabeth stared at the ground and shook her head. "So, that is why you snatched up my husband's business? Did you actually think that holding his money over my head would entice me to marry you?" she asked angrily.

"What? No! I purchased Lansing Wheel to protect your interests, not my own."

Her eyebrows knit over confused eyes. "I–I don't understand."

"Those fools your husband partnered with had no business sense. They would have run the company into the ground, and your investment along with it. I bought it to protect the money your husband invested."

Elizabeth's wrinkled brow furrowed even deeper as Winston Mallory explained what he had done with the business. He told of how he had invested some of his own money and doubled the size of the company over the past thirteen years.

"Lansing Wheel is a very profitable company, Elizabeth, and you own half of it."

"I–I own it? Are you saying that if I marry you, I will actually become part owner?"

"No, that isn't what I am saying at all. It is yours, fifty percent of the business, whether you ever speak to me again or not. Whether you forgive my stupidity or not. It is yours. Elizabeth, you are a very wealthy woman."

ANNA WIPED the tears from her cheeks as she watched her mother. She still was not over the shock of what she had learned when Warren took her to see his father, so she knew it would take her mother some time to process the news as well. It had been his love for her, not his own selfish desires, that had prompted Winston Mallory's actions. Only, cruel fate and misunderstandings had prevented him from following through with his plan. Anna couldn't help but think that, this very day, misunderstandings almost took her from her mother…and from Warren.

Elizabeth's legs began to buckle beneath her. Anna started toward her mother, but Winston was already there, helping her back to the bench. Anna, concerned for her mother, turned anxious eyes to Warren. He was smiling that boyishly handsome smile down at her.

"I told you I knew far more than you realized," he said. He placed her hand in the crook of his arm and led her away from her mother and his father. He turned down a path lined with lilac bushes.

"My mother needs me," Anna protested. But even as she spoke the words, she could see Winston Mallory bring her mother's hands to his cheek and saw that her mother did nothing to resist the affectionate gesture.

"I think we should give them a few moments alone," Warren said.

Anna looked up at him as they rounded the corner of a path that led them deeper into the bushes and out of sight of not only her mother, but other park visitors as well. "You do? Tell me, Warren. Is it their privacy you are concerned with, or our own?" she said, smiling at him coyly.

Warren laughed. "Am I so transparent?"

"Well, this is the only path guarded by seven foot bushes."

Warren swung Anna around to face him and wrapped his arms around her waist.

"Are you ready to answer my question yet?" he asked.

"Question?"

"My father, your mother, they are no longer excuses. So, my question is, are you in love with me, Annabelle Grace Gibson?"

"What's your middle name?"

"What?" he said, pulling back and frowning at her.

"What is your middle name?"

"What does that have to do—"

"You have to tell me if you want my answer," she said, raising her eyebrows.

Warren sighed. "Easy enough, I suppose. It's Edward."

"Like the King of England?"

"Well, yes, I suppose so, although he was still a prince when I was born."

Anna smiled as she slid her arms around Warren's neck. "Mmmm, yes. A prince. That is very fitting. Alright, my prince. Ask me again."

Warren laughed. "Annabelle Grace Gibson, are you in love with me?"

"Warren Edward Mallory, I fell sheepishly in love with the boy who had a tea party with a precocious little girl, and I fell hopelessly in love with the man who chased the misled woman until she could run no further."

Warren brushed his lips against hers softly. "And will you love me, even when I am old and gray?"

"Until I take my last breath," she breathed against his mouth.

A bird fluttered out of a nearby bush, sending the scent of lilacs wafting over them as Warren took her lips into a full kiss. Her pulse quickened and Anna reveled in the knowledge that, from this day forward, the only running left in her life would be the racing of her heart each time she kissed the man she loved.

Sometimes, bad things happen to good people. But sometimes, those bad things are just the beginning of God's plan, a plan for all things to work together, for His purpose, for those who love Him.

Coming May 2019

CHAPTER ONE

WOUNDED

Chateau-Thierry June 1918
  "That was easy."

Everything moved in slow motion as John's bayonet sliced through the chest of the German soldier. He had expected there to be more resistance, what with the thick wool service coat the soldier wore, not to mention the layers of skin, muscle and bone found underneath. But the weapon met with little more resistance than the grain-filled burlap sacks used for training back in the States. The thought was sobering. John's own uniform would not offer any more protection.

Thoughts often outrun actions. The body hadn't even hit the ground before John had finished his musings. *"Another corpse for rotting, along with all the rest."*

He heard the grunt first, then felt the blow. Something – no, someone – hit him in the calves and sent him face down into the dirt. He felt no pain. John scrambled back to his feet just in time to see Will bring his bayonet down into the chest of another German. *"Good,"* John thought. *"Will's still alive."*

This strange internal conversation continued, void of all emotion, while his external being continued the onslaught. How many men had he taken down? He had no idea. He just focused on one at a time, not stopping to think about the one before or the one coming after. Not until an enemy's blade sliced through his left bicep did John snap out of it. Fear at how close the weapon had come to its intended target quickly turned to anger. With a growl, John swung his rifle around. The German had raised his again, intent on finishing his mission, but John was quicker. He thrust his bayonet upward into the enemy soldier's middle. It stuck, but John did not give up. He doubled his efforts, creating so much force that he lifted the man off the ground as the blade finally sliced through his chest.

It was the first his bayonet had met with resistance. And it was the first time he had looked at the face of his enemy.

"My God! He's just a child," John thought. He had to have been younger than Will.

The German, eyes wide, stared in disbelief at John. Both faces, only inches apart, grew pale – one from losing his life, the other from taking it.

John grabbed the front of the falling boy's uniform and gently lowered him to the ground. He stood mesmerized, no longer emotionally disengaged from the act of killing.

He didn't hear the German behind him, nor did he feel the

pain at first. He only felt the pressure as the bayonet slipped easily through the fabric of his doughboy uniform, piercing his skin and pushing deep into his body. He fell forward and landed face to face with the young German boy's body. Fitting, he thought, that this would be his dying view.

Something moved, and he rolled to see a German soldier standing over him with his rifle aimed at John's head. He was powerless to defend himself. He closed his eyes and waited. They were surrounded by gunfire. He doubted he would hear the shot, but surely, he would feel it, unless death were merciful and came quickly. He waited, but no pain came, just a loud grunt and the weight of another man falling on him. Before John could wrap his mind around what was happening, Will was there, lifting the body off of John.

"Can you walk?"

Could he? He wasn't sure. Walk where?

"Stay with me, Johnny!"

Johnny. That's what his mother used to call him. Before she left.

He was drifting, to where, he wasn't sure, but the noise of rifles and grenades began to fade somewhere off in the distance. He felt nothing...

But then, it returned – pain. A searing pain like he had never experienced before shot through his lower back as Will hoisted him onto his shoulders. John was completely back to reality now.

"Leave me, Will," he pleaded. "You'll get yourself killed."

Will ran, hunkered down, with John on his back. The jostling caused so much pain that John began to beg.

"Please Will, just let me die."

Will tripped and stumbled, landing on his knees between two rotting corpses.

"You are going to get yourself killed. Leave me."

"No. I won't leave you," Will said. "We live together, or we die together. But I won't leave you behind."

Will continued his path toward safety. John opened his eyes and could see the bunker just feet ahead. Safety was within reach. But a noise – like a large, metallic mosquito – buzzed past him. Will made a strange sound, then stumbled, and he and John fell, head over heels, down the inside wall of the trench. The last thing John saw was Will, face down in the sludge of the trench, blood pouring from his head.

"We die together," John said, then his world went black.

∽

Lansing, Michigan June 1918

Her father would kill her if he ever found out, but she had to see for herself. The knife-like pressure in her chest was too much to bear. If she were to be cut, then she would be the one to thrust the blade.

Her hand trembled as she knocked – one, two, pause – three. A rustling on the other side of the door and then it creaked open. A large man with a little mustache appeared in the frame.

"Lil' missy, I believe you have the wrong door."

"Dub sent me."

The man's thick eyebrows shot up. "Dub? You don't look like no girl Dub would know."

She was a terrible liar and her confidence began to waiver under the man's scrutiny.

"Well, are you going to let me in?" she asked, trying to maintain her composure.

He eyed her one last time then shrugged his shoulders.

"What do I care who sent ya, as long as ya got money to spend. C'mon in, missy."

She stepped through the door and found herself in a small, windowless room with only a table and a couple of chairs. Fear seized her for a moment as the man shut the door behind her, leaving the two of them alone in the dimly lit room. But within a moment, a door to the back opened and she was ushered into a much larger room full of people.

She quickly looked around. She hadn't expected there to be this many people gathered in an illegal drinking establishment in the middle of the day, but she was having a hard time finding the man she sought amongst the crowd of people gathered here. The thick fog of cigarette smoke wasn't helping the situation.

"Speakeasy?" she muttered under her breath. "There's nothing easy about this."

Worse than having to scan the dark room for the familiar face was having to suffer through the looks she was receiving from the patrons of the seedy establishment. Everyone was eyeing her suspiciously – everyone, that is, that wasn't face down on the table drunk or absorbed in a game of cards.

"You lookin' for someone?"

She breathed in sharply as she spun toward the voice. She hadn't realized the doorman had followed her into the bar.

"Uh, no, I mean – yes, but I don't see..."

But then she did see. Sitting in a front corner booth, with his hand half-way up the skirt of another woman, sat her fiancé.

Anger replaced trepidation as she pushed the burly door keeper out of her way. She marched to the table but stopped short. Her fists clenched, her body trembled, but she said nothing. A hundred words swirled her tongue, but her lips could voice none of them.

The woman noticed her first. Surprisingly, she actually appeared embarrassed. *'Do prostitutes experience such emotions?'* she thought.

The woman pushed away from Richard and pushed her skirt down.

"What's a matter, baby?"

The answer came in the form of an engagement ring hitting his head.

"Esther!" he cried, toppling the other woman to the floor in his haste to leave the table. "It's not what you think!"

But Esther was already halfway to the door, determined to distance herself from the scene of dishonor. She rushed through the two doors and into the waiting car before Richard could untangle himself and reach her. She heard him calling her name as the cab pulled away, but she never looked back.

She clutched her heaving chest, certain that she would find an actual dagger there, slicing her heart in half. But there was no real blade, and no blood gushed from the spot, only the painful striking of her heart against her ribs. She looked up toward the heavens.

"Why does this keep happening to me?"

CHAPTER TWO

Still Alive, Barely

He wasn't dead. The searing pain radiating throughout his lower extremities told him that. But he didn't quite feel alive, either.

How many days had he been here? Two? Three? A week, maybe? John didn't know. He didn't even know where he was. He spent most of the day slipping in and out of a fog of consciousness, but he had noticed windows at one of his more lucid moments. Light streamed through them, making the thunder in his head beat even more painfully, but the colorful display the light produced didn't make sense to him. A constant rainbow? More likely a hallucination.

Doctors had come and gone several times. John had heard much of the same words over and over – tendon damage, severed muscles, spinal something, lucky. Something about barely missing his spine. A few inches to the right, the injury would have left him paralyzed. As it was, though, he would walk again. He heard talk of therapy and of hard work, but he distinctly heard someone say he would walk.

"Ward. Johnathon Ward? Can you hear me?"

John stirred in his bed and tried to focus on the man speaking to him.

"I'm Lieutenant Doherty," said a man in a white coat hovering over John's bed. "You gave us quite a scare at first, but you are going to be all right. You've been under heavy sedation, so your body could heal better, but we're going to start to reduce your pain medication now. Need to get you sitting up and moving a little. Do you understand what I'm saying?"

John blinked, but only the man's mustache and receding hairline were discernible to him. John nodded his head.

"Good. I'll be back in a few hours to check on you and see how much mobility you have."

The doctor patted his shoulder then turned to leave. He stopped at the foot of the bed to speak with someone sitting there. John concentrated on the figure despite the drug induced fog still affecting his vision. He could tell that it was another injured soldier, apparent by the bandage wrapped around his head, but he was too far away to make out anything else. The doctor walked away, and John watched as the man pulled something out of his pocket and rolled it around in his hand.

"Will," he breathed, dropping his head back on the pillow. Relief flooded his veins. Will Caffey was alive.

At the sound of John's voice, Will jumped and pulled his chair to the head of the bed.

"Glad to see you awake, John. I was beginning to worry."

"You were worried?" John groaned. "What about me? Last time I saw you, you were face down with a hole in your head."

Will smirked and touched his bandage. "Just a flesh wound. They say they'll have me back in the trenches in a couple of weeks."

"Hmmph, I wonder how long before they're sending me back?"

Will half chuckled and shook his head. He looked at his hand and started rolling a marble around his palm.

John tried to sit up. Fire emanated from his back and shot down his right leg. He swore under his breath.

Will laughed.

"You think this is funny?" John winced, swearing again.

"Your medication is wearing off. They've kept you pretty drugged up until now."

John let out a long sigh as he straightened himself back onto the bed. "It didn't hurt this bad when it first happened."

"You were still in shock, I imagine."

He nodded his head. He probably had been in shock. They probably all had been in shock since they first stepped onto French ground. He turned his head toward his friend.

"What's the deal with the marble? You always have it with you?"

"It's an aggie," he answered, shrugging his shoulders. "And it belonged to her."

"Ah, I see," John smirked. "Your girl back home that isn't actually yours."

"Her name is Phoebe," Will chuckled. "Phoebe Albright. And she'll be mine someday − if I ever make it home."

"She must be pretty special," John said, with a hint of cynicism.

"She is."

"And beautiful?"

"The most."

"Aren't they all," John chuckled.

"Why do you hate women so much?" Will asked, aggie paused mid-roll.

"I don't hate women. They fulfill a very important role in society. They fill certain − needs," John said with a wink.

Will's jaw clenched, and he returned to the business of rolling the aggie between his fingers. John had gone too far, and he knew it. He squeezed his eyes shut and took a deep breath. He liked the kid, really, he did. He even kind of respected the dedication he had for his religion. They were so different, these two men. But somehow, they had hit it off from the first days of training at Camp Funston. John had taken a liking to the young soldier, seven years his junior. Will Caffey was a fascinating mixture of childlike innocence – an innocence he seemed to carry into every situation, including battle – and a maturity far beyond his years that was present at the same time. With Will, the glass was always half full, and his easygoing smile and good-natured humor almost made John feel as if his glass should be half full as well.

In the early days, John had worried about Will. He worried that the toils of war would wear away at the pureness of the young man. John may be distrustful and cynical, but something in him wanted to keep Will from becoming like him, to keep his innocence intact. However, rather than ruin him, the battlefield seemed to have cultivated Will into a greater man. He had proven his marksmanship during their training days in Kansas, but on the field, it became apparent that the boy had exceptional talent with a rifle. And despite the fact that John was five inches taller, Will was broader through the shoulders and every bit as strong. But his physical strength paled in comparison to his inner strength. How many times had John witnessed Will comfort a frightened comrade or pray with a dying soldier during his last moments? Too many to count. Will had witnessed things that would make much older men weep, but, much like John, he seemed stronger because of it.

John opened his eyes and turned his head back toward his friend. Will continued to roll the aggie, but now his eyes were closed.

"You praying again?"

"Me?" Will chuckled. "Always."

"What do you have to pray about now? Life in the trenches, I understand, but here...hey, where are we anyway?"

A slow smile spread across the clean-shaven face of the younger soldier.

"A church. You did say *'over your dead body,'* and you were almost right."

John looked all around the makeshift hospital now, at the rows of cots filled with injured soldiers, the nurses and doctors tending them, and the windows behind them all – the colorful sunshine hallucinations were stained glass. How had he missed it before? A church, of all places. God must have a sense of humor after all.

"I was praying for you."

John looked at Will in shock.

"Didn't you hear the doctor? I'm going to be alright."

"I wasn't praying for your health. Well, not your physical health, anyway."

"Hmmph," John groaned. "Don't waste your time on my spirit, kid. I'm a hopeless cause."

"Psalm 62 says that hope comes from God, if you'll just let your soul find rest in him."

"And then will I profess unto them, I never knew you, depart from me, ye evildoer."

"Now, see, that gives me hope. You know the Bible. It's hidden in your heart, just waiting for you to allow it freedom in your life."

"Hidden in my heart? More like scarred in my flesh," John scowled.

Will's smile faded. "Your father isn't God, John."

"Tell him that," John laughed.

"You're judging your heavenly Father by your earthly father's actions."

"Actions motivated by scripture."

"Scripture distorted by a sinful man."

John didn't respond. Will was wrong, but he didn't want to be the one to educate him about the truths of the world. Another part of that innocence he felt obligated to protect in his young friend. Besides, Will's disillusioned faith was obviously helping him survive this disgusting war. Let him keep his fantasies. What did it matter to John?

A MESSAGE FROM JEN

❧

Searching for Anna was only intended to be a short story. In the winter of 2017, Gina, one of the members of my writing group, proposed an exercise, wherein we would each write a short including the same handful of words. I agreed, half-heartedly, because I was new to the group and didn't want the popular kids to think I was a dweeb. (Okay, I understand that I am a dweeb just for saying that.) Seriously, though, I DID NOT want to waste my time writing a short story that would not further my career. I had a novel to finish, for goodness sake! But, I did it anyway. Gina can be very convincing. She threatened bodily harm and I caved. (Ed. Note: she did not, though she might after reading this paragraph.)

Honestly, I didn't think much would come of this stupid writing assignment. But, somewhere between 'I hate this idea' and 'I kind of like this Warren guy,' I found the story of a poor seamstress that finds love at the theater. This is the thread from whence was woven the story you hold in your hands right now. Thank you, Gina, for pushing me beyond my comfort zone, for resisting the urge to follow through on physical threats, and to randomly run out of gas while I read rough drafts to you. Haha-haha-ouch, my friend.

One of the words in that writing prompt was the word "Theater." I hadn't planned on ever writing a book about a theater, but Gina made me do it (see above paragraph.) While researching, I found that Lansing, Michigan did in fact have a vibrant, fairly extensive theater district during World War I, the time period in which this series is set. Suddenly, I had found a home for these new characters that I was now in love with... in the series I was already writing! Happy dance!

Sadly, most of Lansing's Theater district is now gone, including the Gladmer, which today is nothing more than a small parking lot that sits on the corner of Washington Avenue and Ionia Street. You heard me correctly...A PARKING LOT! The Gladmer Theater was a beautiful piece of architecture (don't believe me? Google it. It was gorgeous.) But although this loss of a piece of Michigan history really saddened me, it became an even stronger catalyst for me to tell a story that showcased the people and places of this long-gone era of the city of Lansing.

Although the Mallory and Gibson families are completely fictional, I did use real life people and events as inspiration. Lansing, like much of the lower peninsula of Michigan, was built largely by the automobile industry. Henry Ford may be the first Michigander who comes to mind when you think of the dawn of the automobile, but it was Ransom E. Olds and his brands, including Oldsmobile, that put Lansing on the map. Lansing was also the home to many businesses that relied on the automobile industry, including companies like the fictitious Lansing Wheel Company.

In modern society, the idea that Elizabeth Gibson would lose her husband's fortune because there was no will in place might seem ridiculous, but it is based in fact. Katharine Gibbs, founder of Gibbs College, had to apply to the probate court to take control of her late husband's estate. Even more ridiculous… she had to petition the court to be the guardian of her own sons! In my research, I found many stories like hers, of women left destitute and without rights just because their husbands had died without wills. Like Mrs. Gibbs, Elizabeth Gibson found a way to provide for her family, in spite of her circumstances. Although a minor character, Elizabeth is in many ways the hero of this story!

I hope you have enjoyed reading *Searching for Anna* as much as I have enjoyed writing Anna and Warren's story. If you are sad that the story is over, don't fret! Both Anna and Warren make an appearance in future books of my Love in Lansing series, including Book 2: *Avoiding Esther*, releasing in May 2019!

In His service,

Jen

ACKNOWLEDGMENTS

To my God, the true author of not only my life story, but every story I write. I don't think I'll ever understand what You see in me, or why You entrust me with these gifts, but I pray that I have done justice to the story You wanted written.

To my husband and my children. No one knows the sacrifices a family of an author makes. Thank you for loving and encouraging me every step of the way. Thank you for forgiving me when my job as wife and mother took a backseat to my writing. I know it hasn't always been easy, but you never faltered in your support of my dream and I will never forget that. I love you all more than words can say. You are my world.

To Mom and Dad, I never thought you could top your "Parents of the Year" status. That is, until you became grandparents. Thank you for the unlimited babysitting, transportation, feeding and love that you give my girls. This novella would never have happened without all the help you give.

To the ladies of the FLAWS writing group, J.R. Nichols,

Christina Cattane, Rhonda Hagerman, Vicki Hughes, Gina Fender and Barbara Bouck. Without you, there would be no *Anna*. Thank you for your encouragement, the accountability, but most importantly, your friendship.

To Matt Nollen, whose keen eye and hard work kept me from embarrassing myself by publishing a sub-par novella. Your editing skills are matched by none. Keep writing, my friend, because I can't wait to repay the favor!

To Amy Pigott, who so graciously let me call upon her British authority to ensure that Elizabeth and Jameson did not sound too American.

To Ty Brewer: It has been such a joy to watch you grow into such an amazing woman. Having you as the model for the cover means so much to me. I cannot imagine anyone else portraying Anna.

And finally, but definitely not least, to Cheryl Tuttle, the real-life amber eyed beauty in my life. Your friendship and constant encouragement from day one of this journey has helped me to realize that writing wasn't just a dream, but a reality within my reach. You are an inspiration, stronger than you realize, and loved more than words can say.

ABOUT THE AUTHOR

Jenifer Carll-Tong is the author of historical Christian romances. She is a graduate of Boston University's College of Communication. Searching for Anna is her debut novel.

Jenifer lives in Michigan with her handsome husband, three beautiful daughters and two lazy dogs. She also has three adult stepchildren who have left the nest, but not her heart. When she isn't writing kissing scenes between devilishly handsome heroes and strong, independent heroines, you might find her napping or wearing sandals in the snow. You probably won't find her cleaning her house. Unless company is coming over.

Learn more about Jenifer and her books HERE or you can join the fun over at Jenifer's Facebook group, Jenifer Carll-Tong's C.I.R.C.L.E. of Readers. (Heads up…that's where the give-aways happen.)

And don't forget to sign up for her newsletter to stay up to date on the latest news and releases. Visit https://goo.gl/Qur2sU and you will also receive the Searching for Anna ebook absolutely free for signing up!

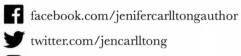

facebook.com/jenifercarlltongauthor

twitter.com/jencarlltong

instagram.com/jencarlltong